ROSE

WITHDRAWN FROM STOCK

HOLLY WEBB

ORCHARD

ORCHARD BOOKS

First published in Great Britain in 2009 by Orchard Books
This edition published in 2017 by The Watts Publishing Group

23

Text copyright © Holly Webb, 2009

The moral right of the author has been asserted.

A CIP catalogue record for this book
is available from the British Library.

ISBN 978 1 40830 447 1

Printed and bound in Great Britain by
Clays Ltd, Elcograf S.p.A.

The paper and board used in this book are
made from wood from responsible sources.

MIX
Paper from
responsible sources
FSC® C104740

Orchard Books
An imprint of
Hachette Children's Group
Part of The Watts Publishing Group Limited
Carmelite House
50 Victoria Embankment
London EC4Y 0DZ

An Hachette UK Company
www.hachette.co.uk

www.hachettechildrens.co.uk

For Jon

ONE

Rose peered out of the corner of the window at the street below, watching interestedly as two little girls walked past with their nursemaid. They were beautifully dressed in matching pale pink coats, and she found them fascinating. How could anyone keep a pink coat clean? She supposed they just weren't allowed to see dirt, ever. The little girls strolled sedately down the street, and Rose stretched up on tiptoe to get one last look as they turned the corner. The bucket she was standing on rocked and clattered alarmingly, and she jumped down in a hurry, hoping no one had heard. The tiny, leaded windows at St Bridget's Home for Abandoned Girls were all very high up, so that the girls were not tempted to look out of them. If any of the matrons realised that Rose had discovered a way to see out, they would do their utmost to stop her, in case her virtue was put at risk by the view of the street. Perhaps they would even outlaw buckets, just in case.

Rose straightened her brown cotton pinafore, and trotted briskly along the deserted passageway to the storeroom to return the bucket. She stowed it carefully on one of the racks of wooden shelves, which was covered in more buckets, brushes and cloths. If anyone saw her, she was planning to say that she had been polishing it.

'Pssst! Rose!' A whisper caught her as she headed for the storeroom door, and Rose shot round, her back against the wall, still nervous.

A small greyish hand beckoned to her from under the bottom shelf, behind a large tin bath. 'Come and see!'

Rose took a deep breath, her heartbeat slowing again. No one had seen her unauthorised use of the bucket. It was only Maisie. 'What are you *doing* under there?' she asked, casting a worried look at the door. 'You'll get in trouble. Come on out.'

'Look,' the whispery voice pleaded, and the greyish fingers dangled something tempting out from under the shelf.

'Oh, Maisie.' Rose sighed. 'I've seen it before, you

know. You showed it to me last week.' But she still crouched down, and wriggled herself under the shelf with her friend.

It was Sunday afternoon. At St Bridget's that meant many of the girls had been in Miss Lockwood's parlour, viewing the Relics. Rose didn't have any Relics, which was why it was a good time for borrowing buckets. Even if anyone saw her, they would probably be too full of silly dreams to care.

'Do you think it's meant to hold a lock of hair?' Maisie asked wistfully. 'Or perhaps a likeness?'

Rose stared thoughtfully at the battered tin locket. It looked as though it had been trodden on, and possibly buried in something nasty, but it was Maisie's most treasured possession – her only possession, for even her clothes were only lent.

'Oh, a likeness, I'm sure,' she told Maisie firmly, wrapping an arm round her friend's bony shoulder. Really she had no idea, but she knew Maisie dreamed about that locket all week, and the hour on Sunday when she got to hold it was her most special time, and Rose couldn't spoil it for her.

'Maybe of my mother. Or perhaps it was hers, and she had my father's picture in it. Yes, that would have been it. I bet he was handsome,' Maisie said dreamily.

'Mmmm,' Rose murmured diplomatically. Maisie

9

wasn't ugly, exactly, but she was very skinny, and no one looked beautiful with their hair cropped short in case of lice. It was hard to imagine either of her parents as handsome.

All Rose's friends spent Sundays in a dream world, where they were the long-lost daughters of dukes who would one day sweep them away in a coach-and-four to reclaim their rightful inheritance.

Strangely though, unlike all the other girls, Rose did not dream. She had no Relic to hang her dreams on, but that wasn't the main reason. Quite a few of the others didn't either, and it didn't hold them back at all. Rose just wanted to get out of St Bridget's as soon as she possibly could. It wasn't that it was a bad place – the schoolmistress read them lots of improving books about children who weren't lucky enough to have a Home. They lived on the streets, and always went from Bad to Worse in ways that were never very clearly explained. Girls at St Bridget's were fed, even though there was never enough food to actually feel full, only just enough to keep them going. They had clothes, even a set of Sunday best for church, and the yearly photograph. The important thing was, they were trained for domestic service, so that when they were old enough they could earn their own living. If Rose dreamed at all, that was what she dreamed of. She didn't want to be a lady in a big house. She'd settle for being allowed to clean one, and be paid for it. And perhaps have an afternoon off, once a month, although she had no idea what she would do.

Occasionally, girls who'd left St Bridget's came back to show themselves off. They told giggly tales of being admired by the second footman, and they had smart outfits that hadn't been worn by six other girls before them, like Rose's black Sunday dress and coat. She knew because the other girls' names had been sewn in at the top. Two of them even had surnames, which was very grand. Rose was only Rose, and that was because the yellow rose in Miss Lockwood's tiny garden had started to flower on the day she'd been brought to St Bridget's by the vicar. He'd found her in the churchyard, sitting on the war memorial in a fishbasket, and howling. If Rose had been given to dreaming like the others, she might have thought that it meant her father had been a brave soldier, killed in a heroic charge, and that her dying mother couldn't look after her and had left her on the war memorial, hoping that someone would care for a poor soldier's child. As it was, she'd decided her family probably had something to do with fish.

Rose hated fish. Although of course in an orphanage, you ate what there was, and anyone else's if you got half a chance. She knew no grand lady was going to sweep into the orphanage and claim her as a long-lost daughter. It must have been a bad year for fish, that was all. It didn't bother her, and just made her all the more determined to make a life for herself outside.

'What do you think they were like?' Maisie asked pleadingly. Rose was good at storytelling. Somehow her stories lit up the dark corners of the orphanage where they hid to tell them.

Rose sighed. She was tired, but Maisie looked so hopeful. She settled herself as comfortably as she could under the shelf, tucking her dress under her feet to keep warm. The storeroom was damp and chilly, and smelled of wet cleaning cloths. She stared dreamily at the side of the tin bath, glistening in the shadows. 'You were two, weren't you, when you came to St Bridget's?' she murmured. 'So you were old enough to be running about everywhere... Yes. It was a Sunday, and your parents had taken you to the park to sail your boat in the fountain.'

'A boat!' Maisie agreed blissfully.

'Yes, with white sails, and ropes so you could make the sails work, just like real ones.' Rose was remembering the illustrations from *Morally Instructive Tales for the Nursery*, which was one of the books in the schoolroom. The two little boys who owned the boat in the original story fought about who got to sail it first, which obviously meant that one of them drowned in the fountain. Most of the books in the schoolroom had endings like that. Rose quite enjoyed working out the exact point when the characters were beyond hope. It was usually when they'd lied to get more jam.

'You were wearing your best pink coat, but your mother didn't mind if you got it wet.' Rose's voice became rather doubtful here. She hadn't been able to resist putting in the pink coat but really, it was too silly…

Suddenly she realised that Maisie was gazing longingly at the side of the tin bath. 'Yes, look, it's got flower-shaped buttons! Are they roses, Rose?'

Rose gulped. 'I'm not sure,' she murmured, staring wide-eyed at the picture flickering on the metal. 'Daisies, I think…' Had she done that? She knew her stories were good – she was always being bothered for them, so they must be – but none of them had ever come with pictures. Pictures that *moved*. A tiny, plump, pretty Maisie was jumping and clapping as a nattily dressed gentleman blew her boat across a sparkling fountain. *White trousers!* Rose's matter-of-fact side thought disgustedly. *Has this family no sense?*

'Oh, the picture's fading! No, no, bring it back, Rose! I want to see my mother!' Maisie wailed.

'Ssssh! We aren't meant to be here, Maisie, we'll be caught.'

Maisie wasn't listening. 'Oh, Rose, it was so pretty! *I* was so pretty! I want to see it again—'

'Girls!' A sharp voice cut her off. 'What are you doing in here? Come out at once!'

Rose jumped and hit her head on the shelf. The picture promptly disappeared altogether, and Maisie burst into tears.

'Come out of there! Who is that? Rose? And you, Maisie! What on earth are you doing?'

Rose struggled out, trying not to cry herself. Her head really *hurt*, a horrible sharp throbbing that made her feel sick. Of all the stupid things to do! This was what happened when you started making pictures on baths. Miss Lockwood looked irritable. 'Maisie, you know you're not supposed to take that out of my office,' she snapped, reaching down and seizing the locket. The flimsy chain broke, and Maisie howled even louder, tugging at the trailing end.

Rose could tell that Miss Lockwood was horrified. She really hadn't meant to snap the locket, and she knew how Maisie treasured it. But she couldn't draw back now. 'Silly girl! Now you've broken it. Well, it's just what you deserve.' Red in the face, she stuffed it into the little hanging pocket she wore on her belt, and swept out. 'Go to bed at once! There will be no supper for either of you!' she announced grandly at the door.

'Well, that's no great loss,' Rose muttered, putting an arm round Maisie, who was crying in great heaving gulps.

'She – broke – my – locket!'

'Yes,' Rose admitted gently. 'Yes, she did. But I'm sure we can mend it. Next Sunday. I'll help, Maisie, I promise. And I don't think she meant to. I think she was sorry, Maisie. She could have made us stand in the schoolroom with books on our heads all evening, like she did to Florence last week. No supper's not that bad. It would only be bread and milk.'

'It might not be,' sniffed Maisie, who seemed determined to look on the black side of things. 'It might be cake.'

Rose took her hand as they trailed dismally back to their dormitory. 'Maisie, it's *always* bread and milk! The last time we had cake was for the coronation, nearly three years ago!' Rose sighed. She couldn't help feeling cross with Maisie for getting her into trouble, but not *very* cross. After all, she'd been tempting fate with the windows anyway. Maisie was so tiny and fragile that Rose always felt sorry for her. 'Do you want me to tell you a story?' she asked resignedly, as they changed into their nightclothes.

'Will you make the pictures come again?' Maisie asked, her eyes lighting up.

15

'I don't know,' Rose told her honestly. 'It's never happened before. And there might be trouble if we get caught, I'm sure it's not allowed.'

'It isn't in the Rules,' Maisie said, pouting. 'I know it isn't.'

Miss Lockwood read the Rules on Sundays before church, so they'd heard them that morning. Rose had to admit that Maisie was right, she didn't remember a rule about making pictures on baths. Which was odd – it must mean that it wasn't a very common thing to do, because the Rules covered *everything*. Even the exact length of an orphan's fingernails.

'It just feels like something that wouldn't be allowed…' Rose said. *Which is why it's such fun*, part of her wanted to add. 'Oh, all right. But I think it needs something shiny for it to work.' She looked round thoughtfully. The dormitory was long and narrow, high up in the attics of the old house. Everything was very clean, but shiny was in short supply. There was hardly room for the girls to move between the narrow, grey-blanketed beds, let alone space for polished furniture.

Maisie followed her, craning her neck to peer into corners. 'My boots are shiny!' she suggested brightly.

Rose was about to say they couldn't be, then realised that Maisie was right. All the girls' shoes were made and mended by the boys from St Bartholomew's orphanage over the wall. They had a cobblers' workshop where the girls had a laundry, so that they could be trained up for a useful trade. Maisie's boots had just come back from being mended, and they were black and shiny, even if they'd been patched so often that there was nothing left of the original boot. If she could make pictures on a bath, why not a boot?

The two girls sat huddled together under Rose's blankets, staring at the polished leather. 'It'll be a lot smaller, if it even works,' Rose warned.

'I don't mind.' Maisie didn't take her eyes off the boot. 'I want to see what happened.'

'It isn't really what happened...' Rose reminded her. 'Just a story I'm making up, you know that, don't you?'

'Yes, yes.' Maisie flapped her hand at Rose irritably, but Rose didn't think she was really listening. 'Show me!'

Long after Maisie had cried herself to sleep that night – heartbroken by the flickering image of her tiny self running through the park and crying for her mother – and the other girls had come chattering to bed, Rose lay awake.

Had she made it all up? It had seemed so real, somehow. *What if I've turned into a fortune-teller?* Rose worried to herself. She didn't *believe* in fortune-tellers. But of course she'd invented it – she'd put in that pink coat, from the little girls she'd seen out of the window. So if it wasn't real, why had it upset Maisie so much? Why had she believed it more than all Rose's other stories? *The pictures*, Rose told herself. *The pictures made it seem too real. I wanted to believe it, too. I'm not doing that again.*

Next to her, Maisie's breath was still catching as she slept, her thin shoulders shuddering, as if she were dreaming it all over again, the lost child that she believed was her, running round the glittering fountain to fetch her boat, then turning back and seeing only other children's parents.

Rose didn't know how she'd done it. This had never happened when she told stories before today. She hadn't done anything differently, not that she could think of. But she must never, ever let it happen again. It was too strong. Rose was sure she'd made it up – or almost sure – but now Maisie had seen it, for her it was real. She would remember it for ever.

Although, Rose thought, as she eventually closed her eyes, *if it were true, the boat would be in Miss Lockwood's office, with the other Relics...* So it couldn't be. It was just a story. But her stories had never frightened her before.

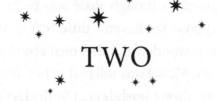

TWO

Rose woke up feeling less cold than usual – the dormitory was always freezing, except for about two weeks in the summer when it was like being roasted. She couldn't work out why, until Maisie wriggled again, and she realised that that was what had woken her.

Maisie's boots were sitting under her bed where Rose had lined them up neatly last night. She stared warily at them, wondering if the pictures would appear again. *Maybe I'll just have to avoid anything shiny*, she thought. *I'll be useless as a housemaid.*

'Will you tell me the story again?' Maisie was leaning up on one elbow, peering down at her.

Rose sat bolt upright and all the blankets fell off. 'No!' Rose shuddered, scrabbling to get them back and

19

keep their hard-won warmth in. 'Of course not!'

'But why?' Maisie pleaded. 'You're so good at it. No one else can do the pictures, Rose, it's beautiful.'

'But you were crying,' Rose reminded her, frowning. 'You cried for ages and ages.'

Maisie shrugged. 'That doesn't mean I didn't enjoy it,' she explained, as though Rose was being dim. She sighed. 'I suppose we haven't time before the others wake up. It was wonderful. I dreamed about it, too.'

Rose thought Maisie was still half in her dream world. Mondays were always washdays at St Bridget's, and she spent the whole morning doing Maisie's work as well as her own. When she caught her friend mangling the skirt she was wearing, Rose made her go and hide behind the big copper and sort stockings, before she did herself an injury. Every girl in the orphanage was wearing odd stockings for the next two weeks, but as it happened, Rose wasn't there to worry about it.

Halfway through the morning, a rustle of interested whispering ran through the laundry. Someone was at the door with Miss Lockwood. A hundred small girls stood on tiptoe, while pretending to keep working. Visitors were rare at St Bridget's, and even if they were only inspecting they were an event. One of the smallest children, four-year-old Lily, was so excited she fell into a washing basket, and had to be hauled out and hidden under a pile of sheets till she'd stopped giggling.

'Is it an inspector, do you think?' someone whispered next to Rose.

'No, no one said an inspector was coming. They always make us wear clean pinafores for inspectors,' an older girl pointed out.

'Maybe it's a benefactor!' Maisie squeaked, from behind the copper. This was very exciting, as the last benefactor had given the girls three bunches of silk roses and a rocking horse, which lived in the schoolroom. Only the littlest ones were allowed to ride it, but everyone was very proud of it, and it had been named Albert, in honour of the king. The roses had mysteriously disappeared.

'She's got a lovely dress on. Black, and a little hat with velvet bits.'

'If she's wearing black she's not a benefactor, she'll be doing Good Works. They always wear black if they're doing Good Works. Not usually a hat that nice though . . .'

The whispering died away as Miss Lockwood and the unknown visitor paced slowly through the laundry. Everyone tried to look busy and hear what they were saying at the same time.

'Of course, we usually like to keep the girls until

they're a bit older…' Miss Lockwood was explaining.

'I do see, but I like to train up my maids myself. I would like a girl of about ten or eleven. Someone sensible.' The lady in the black hat had very bright eyes, Rose saw. She seemed to be noticing everything. She'd spotted Maisie peeking out from behind the copper, and smiled at her. Maisie popped back, scarlet-cheeked.

The whispering started again, much louder, as everyone passed on this fascinating news. She wanted to take someone away! Rose wished she knew exactly how old she was. She was about ten, she was fairly sure. And she knew she was sensible. She tried to look sensible, but she had a horrible feeling she might just look constipated.

Miss Lockwood was gazing thoughtfully round the room. 'Lucy. Ruth. And you, Eliza…'

Rose sighed. She wasn't sensible enough. If only Miss Lockwood hadn't caught them hiding in the storeroom yesterday! For a minute, she truly hated Maisie, but then the flash of anger died away, and she leaned sadly over the mangle, forcing another miserable lump of wet washing through.

'Oh, and perhaps Rose,' Miss Lockwood added. 'Come into my office, girls, so Miss Bridges can look at you.'

Rose gawped at them like a fish, and Maisie and Ellen had to shove her to send her trotting after the others.

It didn't cross Rose's mind that it was strange to be looked over like this, as though the lady in the black hat was out shopping. She just wished that her faded brown dress fitted better. It was tight under her arms. The lady might think she would eat too much. Rose sucked her cheeks in, and tried hard not to think about stories. Miss Lockwood's office seemed to be full of shiny things, and Rose couldn't help seeing herself in them, wearing a smart print frock, and a little white cap.

Miss Bridges walked up and down the little line of orphans. She asked Eliza how old she was, and nodded as Eliza muttered, 'Twelve.' Rose couldn't help thinking that she sounded mulish. *And Lucy doesn't want to be a maid, and Ruth does nothing but giggle. Maybe she'll choose me...*

Then Miss Bridges stopped in front of Rose. 'Are you really ten? You seem very small.'

Rose gulped. 'I think I am,' she replied doubtfully. 'I've been here nine years, Miss, and they thought I was one when I came. I can work,' she added. 'I'm very strong, I really am.' Rose stood on tiptoe, without realising.

'Don't you want to stay in the orphanage?' Miss

Bridges asked curiously. She smiled at Miss Lockwood.

Rose cast her a worried glance as well, and looked between them both as she answered. 'It's not that I don't want to stay,' she murmured. 'But I'd like to earn my own living.'

'Very creditable, dear,' Miss Lockwood reassured her. 'Rose is a good worker, Miss Bridges. A little flighty occasionally, but a good girl.'

Rose's ears turned crimson. Was she? No one had ever said so before.

'Can I take her now?' Miss Bridges asked, rather as if Rose was a new hat.

'Now! Well, I suppose you may.' Miss Lockwood seemed a little shocked. 'Usually we send the girls to their new places with an outfit, and a bible, but I'm afraid we don't have one ready.'

'That will be quite all right,' Miss Bridges said graciously. 'We can supply all she will need. And we can send back her current, er, *outfit*, if it would help.'

'Well, yes…' Miss Lockwood agreed rather helplessly. 'Yes, indeed. Most kind… Now?'

'Now.'

Now! Rose clenched her fists in the skirt of her pinafore to stop herself jumping with excitement. Of course she would miss the others – she didn't want to think of Maisie – but this was what she had been dreaming of, and never expecting.

Lucy's hand crept into hers, and squeezed. 'Good luck!'

Rose smiled at her, but she had a determined little frown on her face. She wasn't planning to let luck have anything to do with it.

Miss Bridges walked fast, and Rose had to scurry to keep up with her. She couldn't help falling behind, for at every step she saw something else new and fascinating. The girls very rarely went out of St Bridget's. Except on Sundays, to church, in a crocodile of a hundred little girls, marching almost in step along the pavement.

Today, however, Miss Bridges had turned right outside the orphanage front door. Rose just stood on the bottom step, staring after her in amazement.

Miss Bridges turned back when she realised Rose wasn't following. 'Are you all right, child? You look worried. Have you changed your mind? I don't want to take you if you're not happy to go.'

Rose shook her head vigorously and jumped off the step, running after her. 'I do want to, I really do. I'm sorry, Miss. It's only that we never go this way.'

Miss Bridges raised her eyebrows. 'What's wrong with this way?'

'Well, nothing, but church is the other way, you see. We only ever go to church,' Rose said simply.

'I hadn't realised.' Miss Bridges looked down at Rose, trotting beside her in her brown dress, and a scratchy grey shawl. Her bonnet was much too small, and it was threatening to fall off at every step. 'Have you really never been anywhere else?'

Rose shook her head. 'Not that I remember, Miss.'

The orphanage was not in a smart area of the town. There were few interesting shops to see, and of course they were never open on a Sunday anyway. But now Miss Bridges was leading Rose into more fashionable streets. It was the middle of a Monday morning, and they were crowded with people shopping, running errands, or just out walking. Rose found them all fascinating, but she couldn't help staring at the children her own age.

'We turn here, into this square.' Miss Bridges swept her round a corner. 'Mr Fountain's house is on the other side, in the corner there.' Rose gazed at the tall, stone houses, their windows sparkling in the sunlight. The centre of the square was a garden, with statues, and three little boys playing with a toy horse. It was very quiet after the busy streets they'd walked through, and Rose wasn't sure she had ever been so close to a tree. 'It's beautiful, Miss,' she said quietly. Then she looked up in surprise. 'Mr Fountain's house? It isn't your house, Miss?'

Miss Bridges laughed. 'I'm just the housekeeper, Rose. You and I both work for Mr Aloysius Fountain, the famous alchemist.'

THREE

Miss Bridges took Rose down what she called the area steps, which led straight into the kitchen in the basement. 'We don't use the front door, you see, that's for the family.'

Rose nodded. The front door was huge, painted dark green with a golden mermaid door knocker, and it was up a flight of marble steps. It was far too grand for her.

The kitchen seemed full of people, sitting round a wooden table on which was an enormous brown china teapot. A plump lady at one end of the table nodded regally. 'A cup of tea, Miss Bridges?'

Miss Bridges nodded back very graciously. 'Thank you, Mrs Jones, that would be most refreshing. This is Rose, the new second housemaid, from the orphanage.

Rose, Mrs Jones is our cook, and has sole charge of the kitchens.'

Rose stared at her boots, aware that everyone else in the kitchen was staring at *her*. Miss Bridges seemed to have become much grander now that she was with these other people, and Rose was too shy to ask who they all were.

'She's very small.' A dark-haired girl a few years older than Rose, wearing a smart apron, sniffed dismissively at her. 'I don't see how she'll be much use.'

'Be quiet, Susan,' snapped the cook. 'A child half her size could do more work than you do, and if she's from St Bridget's she'll know what's what. Go and get on with polishing the silver.'

Susan gave Rose a dirty look and flounced out into the back kitchen.

Miss Bridges pushed Rose gently into a chair. 'If Rose could have a cup of tea, Mrs Jones, then I'll take her to find some dresses. Our last under-housemaid has had to go home to look after her mother, Rose. We'd fit two of you into her dresses, but I'm sure we'll manage something.'

Rose sipped the tea – in a china cup, with a saucer! – and shyly watched the rest of the table. She soon gathered that it was washday here too, and that the lady at the end of the table in at least six shawls and a black straw bonnet was the washerwoman, Mrs Trump. Then there was a kitchen maid, Sarah, and a boy of about fourteen who seemed to be there to do everything else. His name was Bill, and he had short greyish-blond hair and looked a bit like a rat, although a nice one.

'Has anyone told you what the master does yet?' he whispered to Rose.

Rose shook her head worriedly. Miss Bridges had said something, as they arrived, but Rose hadn't understood, and she'd been too embarrassed to ask. It sounded like she'd said he was a chemist, which was like an apothecary, Rose knew. But no apothecary lived in a house like this, so she must have it wrong.

'Is he a doctor?' she asked. She knew doctors were rich.

Bill sniggered, and slurped his tea, which drew him a frown from Miss Bridges. 'Nah. He's an alchemist. Know what that is?'

Rose shook her head. It was the same thing Miss Bridges had said. Maybe it just meant a very good apothecary, but she had a feeling that Bill wanted to be able to tell her, so she didn't guess, just looked wide-eyed and hopeful at him.

'He's a magician.' Bill nodded at her impressively, and Rose stared back. Was he having her on? He didn't look as though he were teasing. Seeing the doubt in her eyes, he nodded again. 'Honest. An alchemist is a magician who can make gold out of nothing.'

Rose scowled. Now she *knew* he was having her on. She hunched her shoulders over her teacup and ignored him.

'Bill is almost right, Rose.' Miss Bridges took a delicate sip of her tea – her cup had flowers, and pink swirls on the handle. 'Mr Fountain can't make gold from thin air, as Bill seems to be suggesting. But he can transform base metals. Lead, for example. He is the Chief Magical Counsellor to the Royal Treasury and the Mint. A very important man.'

'He makes gold?' Rose faltered, still unsure this wasn't some huge joke. She knew about magicians, of course, but she'd never seen one. It would be a bit like seeing a princess. Though magicians were rare and special, and the king had five daughters and a great many cousins, and they all went out and waved at the people a lot. She was far more likely to see a princess, really. But now she was living in a magician's house? Rose shuddered, and peered around the kitchen, suddenly expecting to see a skull, or a stuffed crocodile, or a pan full of newts bubbling on the stove. Her knowledge of magicians was only from the ghost stories that were whispered round the dormitory after dark.

Rose had never really thought that much about

magic before. She knew it existed, of course, but it didn't tend to get mentioned a great deal at St Bridget's. It was incredibly expensive – the sort of luxury that an orphanage would never need, even more so than food that wasn't cabbage. There had been no magic in the orphanage – although some of the older girls swore that Miss Lockwood had a magical glass eye that she kept in her office. Otherwise how did she manage to be so particularly where the girls didn't want her, all the time? Rose was almost sure it was nonsense though. Such a thing would cost an enormous amount of money, far more than the superintendent of an orphanage could afford. Magic was only for rich people, everyone knew that, especially the orphans. Rose had wondered if she'd ever see any when she went into service, but even well-to-do households usually owned only one or two spells, and perhaps an unbreakable dinner service, most often a wedding present.

Rose stared anxiously into the corners, but no stuffed crocodile leered back. Everything looked normal – but then, Rose didn't have a lot of experience of kitchens, even though all the orphans helped in the kitchen at St Bridget's. The huge room had always smelled of boiled cabbage and endless suet puddings, and was full of little girls chopping more cabbage. It was quite a change to be in a kitchen that didn't smell of cabbage at all. This one smelled of tea, and of something sweet and delicious baking in the big black oven. There were pots of geraniums on the windowsill, and a collection of fantastically shaped copper jelly moulds lined the wall. There were bunches of herbs dangling from hooks, but Rose thought they were probably for sage and onion stuffing and suchlike, not for spells.

Mrs Jones smiled approvingly at her suspicious face. 'No magic in my kitchen,' she said firmly. 'Nasty, messy stuff. It never tastes right.'

Rose nodded, wide-eyed. Mrs Jones was so obviously telling the truth. This wasn't some silly joke. She really was in a house full of magic – it just wasn't allowed in the kitchen...

Just then one of the row of brass bells hanging on the wall began to shake and clatter.

'Mr Fountain's study,' Miss Bridges said. 'Hmmm.' She eyed Rose. 'No, I think we'll wait to show you to him until you're tidied up, Rose. I don't want him thinking you're a little ragamuffin. Susan!' she called. 'Leave the silver, and answer the master's bell. I should think he wants tea.'

Rose nodded, and stared at the table, seeing Susan's full black skirt swish past her out of the corner of her eye. A ragamuffin? She supposed she was, but she was so used to seeing everyone at the orphanage in worn, too-small clothes like her own, that she hadn't really thought about it. She swallowed, gulping. Miss Bridges had been so nice – much nicer than a housekeeper might have been, Rose was sure – that it hurt for her to say something so casually rude. Rose wished fiercely that she'd been given time to put her Sunday clothes on – they might be old, but they were beautifully clean, and they almost fitted. She wouldn't have looked quite so bad then.

A calloused hand lifted her chin gently. Mrs Jones was leaning across the table, inspecting her. She nodded encouragingly. 'In a nice print dress, with her hair brushed and a cap, she'll look quite respectable. Don't be crying, Rose dear. Miss Bridges just means you don't show to advantage like you are. Mr Fountain can be a mite fussy.'

Bill sniggered. 'He spends half an hour just doing his hair in the mornings!'

Miss Bridges glared at him. 'As you well know, William Sands, Mr Fountain is a member of His Majesty's Court! He can hardly appear before the king and queen without brushing his hair. And did you brush yours this morning, might I ask?' she enquired glacially. 'It certainly doesn't look like it from here. Finish your tea and go and help with the mangling.'

Rose darted a glance at Bill's hair, feeling better. She wasn't sure you could brush it, it was so short and tufty. It looked a bit like a balding doormat, that same sort of sandy colour. She didn't say anything. It wasn't her place – they'd been very keen on knowing your place at St Bridget's. Miss Lockwood had given them all long lectures on it, and Rose was pretty sure that at the Fountain house, as at the orphanage, her place was the lowest of the low. She definitely needed to keep on Bill's good side, especially as it seemed she'd already offended the other maid, Susan, just by being there.

Bill grinned at her as he slurped up the last of his tea. He didn't seem at all worried about being told off.

'Bill came to us a couple of years ago from St Bartholomew's,' Mrs Jones explained as he swaggered into the scullery. 'It was what made us think of looking for a maid at St Bridget's.'

'Bill is an orphan, too?' Rose asked, surprised. He seemed so confident – so happy.

'Yes, a foundling like yourself. He's been a good worker.' Mrs Jones nodded approvingly. 'Just as I'm sure you will be.'

A few hours later, Rose was doing her best to prove just how hard she could work. She was sitting opposite Bill at a big table in the back kitchen, which seemed to be where all the odd jobs got done. They were polishing the silver, not just knives and forks and things, but great big plates, and cups, all with inscriptions on them in curly letters. They mostly said things like, *To Aloysius Fountain, in grateful admiration, The Worshipful Guild of Rat-Catchers.* That one had little rats prancing all around the edge. Rose couldn't help wondering just what Mr Fountain had done to make them so grateful.

'Do we have to do this every day?' she asked, hoping they didn't.

'Course not,' Bill told her scornfully. 'Once a week.' He checked over his shoulder to see who was listening in the main kitchen. 'And sometimes I don't bother doing all of them,' he hissed. 'No one notices. They don't get used unless there's a party.'

'Mr Fountain gives parties?' Rose was surprised. Everyone had been so eager to tell her what a serious, clever, important man he was, that she couldn't imagine him wanting a party.

'Mmm. For all his grand friends from Court, or other magicians sometimes.'

Rose nodded thoughtfully. 'I suppose he's lonely, living here all on his own,' she offered.

Bill hooted with laughter. 'Who says he lives on his

own, silly? There's Miss Isabella, for starters, and then Mr Freddie.'

'Oh! He's got children. I didn't know.' Rose had thought Mr Fountain was too old to have children. She'd imagined all magicians as old, which she realised now was stupid.

But Bill was shaking his head again. 'Just the one. Miss Isabella. Mrs Fountain died, not long after she was born. Mr Freddie' – his voice was disdainful now – 'he's the master's apprentice.' It was easy to see that Bill was not impressed by Freddie.

'Freddie!' Rose giggled. She thought she was on safe ground here, and sure enough, it earned her an approving look from Bill.

'He's about your age, I reckon. Not got the sense he was born with.' Bill sniffed disgustedly.

'But if he's training to be a magician...' Rose began doubtfully, rubbing at a silver platter engraved with fighting dragons. (Dragons! Were dragons real, too? The orphanage was short on exciting, adventurous sorts of books, but there were one or two that had slipped in because they had boring-looking covers. Dragons definitely came in the same kind of stories as magicians. Rose decided to store this question up for later. She'd had enough of Bill laughing at her.)

'I'm not saying he's stupid, or nothing.' Bill brandished

his polishing cloth fiercely. 'He's very *clever*. But he's the kind who'd fall down the stairs because he forgot they were there.'

Rose gave him a disbelieving look. No one was that silly.

Bill shrugged. 'Last week. I was the one that picked him up, *and* got lumbered with sweeping up all the broken china. He hit a vase on the way down, see. Miss Bridges near had a fit. It was Ming, or something.'

'Was he hurt?' Rose asked worriedly. She didn't know this Freddie, but she didn't like to hear of anyone forgetting a staircase.

'Nope.' Bill sounded disappointed. 'He was pleased. Said he'd almost floated down the last six steps, and he hadn't known he could. In which case he blooming well ought to have floated that vase, that's all I can say.'

'Bill, I hope you're not gossiping to Rose?' Miss Bridges swept in with an armful of dresses. 'Come and see if any of these will fit with a bit of altering, Rose. And I'll show you your room as well.' She sailed out of the room while Rose was still fumbling with the big sacking apron she'd been given, and she had to race after her, glaring at Bill as he sniggered.

'Always the back stairs, remember, Rose, till you get to the first floor, never the main staircase,' Miss Bridges called down as Rose trotted after her. Rose gasped out,

'Yes, Miss Bridges.' She was beginning to think she needed to write a list of things she mustn't do.

Rose's room was right at the top of the house, up at least six flights of stairs. At any rate, it felt like six flights – for some reason she had trouble counting them. And how many doors were there? The house wasn't spooky at all, it was bright, with hundreds of windows that sparkled in the afternoon sunlight, and it was spotlessly clean, which Rose approved of. Not a single cobweb. But there was still something mysterious about it. Something slightly disturbing. Rose tried to tell herself that it was just because she had never been in a house this big or this grand before. But she had a worrying feeling that the strangeness was because up here on the main floors, the walls were positively soaked in magic.

At least her attic room was perfectly normal. The odd, sparkling, shadows-in-your-eyes feeling wore off once they got beyond the carpets. The plain wooden stairs to the servants' rooms were a little dusty, and creaked, and by the time they'd reached the last and tiniest attic bedroom, Rose felt she could breathe again.

Miss Bridges had had to slow down by the fourth staircase. Now she opened the door and sank down gracefully on the little white bed with the bundle of dresses. 'Here you are, Rose,' she said, puffing a little.

'Is this – all for me?' Rose asked, sure that it couldn't be right. 'My own room?'

Miss Bridges smiled. 'Yes. The rooms are too small to share. Susan sleeps next to you, so you can ask her if you need something.'

Rose nodded, though privately she vowed not even to breathe near Susan if she didn't have to. She was well used to tiptoeing around the bigger girls at the orphanage. She smiled to herself, thinking how jealous they would be. Her own room, not shared with anyone! And she was to have four dresses, only one a hand-me-down, so she had something to wear while the new ones were sewn. Even knowing that she would have to do most of the sewing couldn't dim the glory of those dresses.

Miss Bridges left her to put on the lilac print hand-me-down dress, and her apron, reminding her again to come down the back stairs once she got to the main floors. Rose nodded eagerly. She wanted to have just a minute alone in her room – even though it was so small she could almost touch both walls if she stood in the middle, it was *hers*. It had a shelf by the bed for a candle, and hooks for her dresses, and even a tiny looking glass. Rose adjusted the cap in it, trying hard to make it look as smart as Susan's. Then she gave her room one last fond look and set off downstairs.

Rose pattered down the wooden staircase, still in her

patched old boots. As she turned the corner onto the first flight of stairs that might possibly be used by the family, and therefore had carpet, although not the rich plush of the lower floors, she *felt* the difference. The house hummed. It sang in her head. The walls sparkled, and the corridors seemed to stretch for miles. Rose hung tightly on to the banister, feeling as though she might float away on the wobbling stairs. What *was* this place?

'Are you lost?' an amused voice said in her ear. 'You've been standing there for ages.'

Rose squeaked and sat down with a thump on the stairs. She could have sworn the blond-haired boy had appeared from nowhere. Surely there hadn't been anyone there before?

'Who are you?' she gasped, too surprised to remember that servants shouldn't ask impertinent questions.

The boy raised his fair eyebrows, and his voice was rather cold as he replied, 'I am Frederick Paxton.'

Rose stood up quickly, reminded of where she was – and *what* she was – by his sharp tone. 'I'm sorry, Sir, you startled me,' she murmured, bobbing a curtsey. 'I only came today, and – and I can't see my way back to the kitchen, somehow.' She gazed round in confusion. The stairs seemed to look different every time she blinked.

'Follow these stairs down, and then the back stairs,

those for the *servants*, are on the left,' said the boy. It was odd to be spoken to so coldly by someone her own age – someone Rose thought she could fairly easily have taken in a fight.

'Thank you, Sir.' Rose bobbed again, and scuttled away, glancing back only once. The boy was staring after her, and his face was hard to read. He looked disgusted, rather as though she were some sort of beetle, but there was something else. Unless she was very much mistaken, he was also curious. And – possibly – somewhat scared…

FOUR

Rose hadn't been sure what to expect, now that she was working. Would it be harder than the orphanage? At St Bridget's the girls had worked most of each day, with lessons fitted in where they could be. It was felt that as long as the girls could read and write up to a point, they were better off learning to sew, or clean fireplaces. After all, that was what they were going to spend the rest of their lives doing. They would only ever need to read enough to do the shopping.

Rose told herself, that first day, that she didn't mind how difficult the work was. She was free! She was going to be paid – she still found this hard to believe. If the mood came upon her, she could walk out of the house and leave her job, and *no one would be able to stop her.*

The mood wouldn't, of course, but it was nice to know that it could.

Susan woke her at six the next day by slamming open her door and snarling, 'Get up, you. You'll be late.'

Rose sighed. She didn't know late for *what*, and she still wasn't sure what she had done to make Susan dislike her quite so much, but there didn't seem a lot of point in worrying about it. She smiled as Susan stomped back to her own room, and went to the water jug to wash. The lilac print was still pristine, and she and Sarah and Miss Bridges had almost finished sewing a pink-striped cotton between them the previous night.

After her experience with the swaying staircases the day before, Rose had decided that once she got onto the family floors she would just stare at her feet. Hopefully that way she wouldn't be distracted by dancing furniture, unless the carpet started too – it *was* quite fiercely patterned. She managed to get to the door to the servants' stairs with only quick glances out of the corners of her eyes, but nearly impaled herself on an ornamental sword hanging from the wall at stomach height – one that she was sure hadn't been sticking out as much yesterday. She scurried down the back stairs, and flung herself into the kitchen, glad to get there in one piece with no holes.

'Goodness, child, whatever's the matter with you?' exclaimed Mrs Jones, slopping tea into Miss Bridges' saucer and tutting. 'Fetch me a cloth, Sarah, do.'

'I'm sorry, Mrs Jones.' Rose automatically bobbed at the knees in a little half-curtsey. It seemed to appease Mrs Jones, but she clearly still wanted an answer. 'I – it sounds silly – but everything *moves* up there... I was just trying to get down the stairs while they were still there,' she added apologetically.

Miss Bridges peered at her sharply over the rim of her teacup. 'What moves, Rose?'

'The walls. And the stairs... And I'm sure one of the swords jumped at me!'

'You're having us on!' Bill was standing by the back door with the ash bucket, looking disgusted. 'Them stairs have never moved that I've seen.'

'But they did!' Rose pleaded. She didn't want Bill to think she was as silly as Freddie, wittering on about floating down the stairs.

'I wouldn't be surprised, in this house,' Mrs Jones said darkly. 'Not that the stairs would move with *me*.'

Bill smirked, and Rose couldn't help wanting to giggle. The stairs wouldn't dare. She could easily imagine Mrs Jones's reaction to magical furniture. *'Now just you put me down at once, or I'll fetch a feather duster to you!'* Mrs Jones just didn't hold with magic.

45

Rose had a feeling that it was probably the safest way to be. She wished she didn't hold with it either, but it seemed to keep sneaking up on her. She resolved to have nothing to do with it. If anything wobbled, she would just close her eyes.

'You've really never seen anything strange?' Rose asked Bill quietly, as he showed her where to find everything she'd need to light the bedroom fires.

Bill shrugged. 'Nope. The odd explosion, here and there. Mostly when Mr Freddie's mucked something up. He's not very good at this magic lark, seems to me. You're imagining it about the stairs, though. It's just a house. Made of bricks, and…and stuff. How can it *move*?'

Rose nodded sadly. She wished that was true, but she knew she'd seen it. It was going to be difficult if she had to spend all her time looking at her boots.

'Start with Miss Anstruther, that's the governess, on the second floor at the end of the corridor. Opposite the picture of the fat girl with the horse. Then do Mr Freddie and Miss Isabella, and then Mr Fountain. Susan does the downstairs rooms. And be quick or you'll miss breakfast.'

Rose picked up the heavy coal bucket, and the brushes and cloths.

'Don't bang it about like that!' Bill scolded. 'You're

supposed to be silent! You have to not wake them up, don't you get it?'

Rose looked at him worriedly. She knew how to lay a fire, and light it, but how on earth was she supposed to do it without making any noise? Coal was noisy – it was made of rocks, it had to be.

'Oh well.' Bill shrugged. 'They all sleep like the dead anyway. Just do the best you can.'

This certainly seemed to be true of Miss Anstruther. She only turned over and grunted when Rose dropped a cascade of coal all over the hearth, and then said something that would have got her mouth washed out with soap at St Bridget's.

Mr Freddie woke up and glared at her like a ruffled white mouse when she opened his door, but Rose decided she was probably supposed to ignore him. She glanced over her shoulder at him as she scuttled out. He was still watching her, though he shut his eyes as soon as he saw her looking. What *was* he thinking? Rose had a strong feeling that he would quite like to turn her into a beetle.

Rose didn't know an awful lot about boys. She didn't remember ever having spoken to one before Bill. The matrons at St Bridget's were convinced that the orphans' morals would be forever destroyed if they so much as breathed the same air as a boy. They saw the boys from St Bartholomew's on Sundays at church, but that was all. And the orphan boys stayed strictly on their side of the aisle. Even so, she knew what everyone at the orphanage would have said about this one – that he was a spoilt snob who'd never had to lift a finger. They would have taken great pleasure in blacking his eye for him. Both of them, if possible.

Rose shook her head disgustedly. It was a pity not to be able to tell Mr Freddie what she thought of him, but of course she couldn't. She'd be dismissed at once. Besides, there was the possibility of being a beetle, too. At least she had normal, sensible Bill to talk to – she definitely felt the same way about Freddie as he did. A tiny doubt rose somewhere in the region of Rose's stomach, that actually, she wasn't quite normal either. It wasn't normal to be able to make pictures, but at least no one knew about that. She'd made a mistake earlier on, though. None of the rest of the servants could feel the staircases fidgeting under their feet.

Rose resolved to be as normal as she possibly could. Boringly normal, if she could manage it. She simply didn't want anyone to notice her.

She nearly dropped the coal scuttle at her first sight of Miss Isabella's bedroom. From the expressions of the servants when they talked about her, and everyone's huge sympathy for Miss Anstruther (Mrs Jones had made some revolting herb tea for her yesterday, to help her keep her strength up, after screaming had been heard from the direction of the schoolroom), Rose had got the impression that Isabella was rather spoilt. Her bedroom was incredible. Anything that could possibly have lace, had it. The bed had a lace canopy, held up by a smirking golden angel, and was covered in layers of lace-edged pillows and embroidered ruffles. There were dolls and toys everywhere, and a rocking horse even larger than Albert, just for one little girl. Rose peered over at her. Golden curls. Of course. And a very lacy nightie. She couldn't see much else. Rose shook her head in amazement, and remembered breakfast.

She'd better hurry. Goodness, even the fireplace had flowery tiles.

'Who are *you*?' an imperious little voice demanded, and Rose jumped, spraying ash all over the grate. She edged round on her knees, and looked up. Miss Isabella was kneeling up on the end of her bed, staring at her.

'I'm sorry, Miss, I didn't mean to wake you,' Rose murmured. 'I'm the new housemaid, Rose.'

'Oh. You're ugly.' Isabella yawned. 'Lots of coal, please, it's chilly. And pass the biscuits.'

Rose gaped at her for a second, then looked round, and found a pink china biscuit barrel on the bedside table, within easy reach of Isabella's hand. Nevertheless, she got up and offered it to her politely, and Isabella took a huge handful. Rose tried not to look envious; she was hungry too. She finished laying the fire with a biscuit-muffled running commentary from Isabella on how clumsy she was, and how much prettier Lizzie, the last maid, had been. By the time the fire was finally lit, Rose felt like slapping the horrible brat. She shut the bedroom door behind her, and leaned on it, taking a deep, calming breath. Little toad! Was she a magician too? Perhaps she was too young to know much yet. Rose hoped so. She resolved to put extra coal on Miss Anstruther's fire tomorrow – the poor woman deserved it.

Luckily, not even Rose's rumbling stomach woke up Mr Fountain. All she saw of him was a rather elaborate nightcap, and his large moustache. She had to stifle a giggle, as it was held in a strange black net, which fixed over his ears. It looked as though his moustache was taking over his face... But there was nothing else that suggested he was a renowned magician. He snored.

Rose galloped back down the stairs – still carefully not looking at the walls in case they took the opportunity to move at her. Mrs Jones pushed a large bowl of porridge in front of her as she slid into her seat at the table, and Bill passed her a jar of honey. He mumbled something sarcastic about stairs, but Rose couldn't understand it, as his mouth was already stuffed with porridge. Rose set to following his example. It was very good porridge.

Suddenly something silky and furry brushed against Rose's legs and she squeaked in shock, jumping up in her chair.

'Oh, it's that dratted cat again,' Mrs Jones exclaimed, as a silvery blur shot out from under the table. It resolved itself into a handsome, rather portly, white cat, who jumped up onto the table next to Rose, and stared inquisitively into her face. It had one blue eye, and one orange one, and enormous whiskers.

'Not on the table, please, Gustavus!' Miss Bridges said, and Rose looked up at her, surprised. Her voice was very polite, for someone who was telling off a cat. The orphanage cat had been strictly a mouser, and not a pet. He got shouted at a lot, as there were a great many mice, and he probably weighed only half as much as this fine gentleman.

Gustavus – was the cat really called that? – looked at her thoughtfully, and apparently decided to co-operate by sitting on Rose's lap instead. Then he peered hopefully across the table, eyeing the larder door.

'Well, the cat likes you,' Miss Bridges noted. 'That's useful. Susan, fetch that animal a saucer of cream, will you?'

Gustavus's whiskers quivered with excitement, and his tail-tip twitched back and forth against Rose's leg as Susan disappeared huffily into the cool, stone-floored larder.

Rose watched him curiously. 'Does he understand what you say?' she asked, still staring at him.

'He's not natural,' Bill said, and the cat leered at him in a friendly way. Bill shuddered. 'Monster.'

Susan slapped down a gilt-edged saucer in front of Rose, and Gustavus glared at her disapprovingly. The cream had slopped over the edge, and he clearly wasn't happy about it. Susan sat down, and started to eat her porridge, but she only managed one mouthful before she laid the spoon down again. Gustavus was still staring at her.

'Oh, very well!' she snarled, and flounced up to fetch a cloth and wipe away the drops. Once the table was clean again, the cat consented to lap delicately at the cream. His whiskers trailed in it, they were so long. At one point he stopped his luxurious lapping, and turned round to look at Rose. A very deliberate look, such as Rose would have given to one of the other girls who she'd caught staring at her in church. A *What?* look.

'Sorry,' Rose whispered. 'Um. You've got cream on your whiskers...'

And?

Nothing... Rose twitched, suddenly realising that she'd said that silently. Or had she? Surely she was imagining this snippy little conversation with a fat white cat.

Gustavus slowly licked the cream off his whiskers, still staring at her. His tongue was enormously long, and it curled elegantly round his whisker-tips, savouring every drop. Then he turned back to the saucer, and resumed his slow, dignified appreciation of the cream.

'Best Jersey cream...' Mrs Jones muttered to herself, a stricken look in her eyes. 'Wasted on a cat!'

'Gustavus belongs to Mr Fountain, Rose,' Miss Bridges told her. 'Which explains why he is, er, somewhat *indulged*.'

The cat turned back to Rose and winked, with the blue eye.

'He's obviously taken a fancy to little Rose, though,' Mrs Jones put in, still looking at the saucer of cream as though it were painful. 'Someone has to feed him, so...'

'She can brush him too then, if he likes her so much,' Susan snapped. 'He scratches, nasty brute.'

Well, you're popular, Rose told the cat, without thinking.

I wouldn't make a habit of that, dear. Or don't let them see you doing it, anyway.

Rose nodded slightly. The cat was right. She had no idea how she was talking to him, but she could see that there was a definite mistrust of this magical creature among the servants. And none of them seemed to like Freddie much, either. Maybe normal people just didn't trust magic? But then, Miss Bridges clearly thought the world of Mr Fountain, and Bill seemed to have a grudging respect for him, too. He did pay their wages, she supposed. It was difficult to pin down. Still, it would be better not to let slip that she was grasping at the edges of this strange subject. At least until she understood more of what was going on. Magic was clearly an upper-class thing. It wasn't her place to know about it. Rose shuddered. She didn't want to be seen as getting above herself.

She looked up and caught Miss Bridges eyeing her consideringly. Rose tried to look innocent, and rather stupid, but she wasn't sure that Miss Bridges was convinced. Her dark eyes were interested, interested and thoughtful behind the glittering pince-nez spectacles she was using to inspect the laundry list. Rose had a worrying feeling that Miss Bridges didn't believe she was stupid at all.

After breakfast Miss Bridges took Rose on a more thorough tour of the house than she'd had the day before, to show her what her duties were. Like this morning with the fires, it seemed that Susan, as the first housemaid, dealt with the main rooms, the grander ones on the ground floor, and Rose did upstairs. That was fine by her. She'd had a quick peek at the drawing room as they passed, and the number of fragile-looking ornaments had set her heart racing. She would much rather clean bedrooms. It was just about possible to smash a chamber pot if you tried hard enough, but it would take a real effort.

'And this is the workroom.' Miss Bridges opened a smoke-stained door. 'Mr Fountain uses it for magical…things…' she added vaguely. 'But he's always at Court at this hour so you won't be disturbing him. Dust the equipment, sweep the floor, polish the vessels, but for heaven's sake, Rose, do not touch *anything* that he's working on. It could be vital to the nation.'

Rose eyed the piles of delicate glassware anxiously. Perhaps the drawing room wasn't such a bad choice after all. She shivered. The room was gloomy – even though it was surrounded by tall windows. The light just didn't seem to reach into the corners. There were no spiders' webs, and no dust, but it was still an eerie place. The central table was loaded with a complex arrangement of glass tubes and bottles filled with a murky yellow liquid, flowing sluggishly from one end to the other.

'Is that gold?' Rose asked curiously. After all, Bill had *said* Mr Fountain made gold, and gold was yellowish.

'Of course not!' a voice behind her snapped.

The pale-haired boy, Freddie, was standing there looking disgusted.

Miss Bridges sniffed, which was the most unladylike thing Rose had yet seen her do. Clearly Freddie was about as unpopular as the cat, who now prowled into the room behind him, looking smug.

Rose watched him under her eyelashes, while pretending to stare humbly at her boots. She was getting very familiar with them here. Rose had a feeling that it wasn't his magical ability that made Miss Bridges dislike Freddie, more that he was rude. She seemed to have more patience with magic (and the people who could do it) than the rest of the servants. Freddie had recently broken a Ming vase, of course – Miss Bridges had probably wanted him disembowelled for that.

Freddie stalked past her, wrapped in a cloud of *don't touch me* superiority. Rose wished she could ask him about the strange things that had been happening to her recently, and how his own magic worked, but she was meant to be invisible to these people.

Miss Bridges left Rose to it, with another warning against touching things she shouldn't. Freddie settled at a table and started turning the pages of a large book, while the cat sat next to him and stared at Rose as she swept the floor. She could feel his eyes fixed on her. It made her feet feel twice their real size, and she almost tripped over her brush.

'You've missed a bit.' Freddie was peering over the book at the floor, and the cat was examining it too. Neither of them seemed to think Rose's work was up to scratch.

Rose carefully didn't sigh. Instead she just murmured, 'Yes, Sir,' and swept the patch he seemed to be pointing to, which looked perfectly clean to her.

Freddie lifted the book up to sit on its end, so he could snigger behind it, and Rose felt herself flushing angrily. Then she noticed the gold-embossed title on the scuffed black leather cover. *Prendergast's Perfect Primer for the Apprentice Mage.* If only she could look at it! It would surely tell her what to do about odd pictures on baths, dancing houses and talking cats. Preferably, how to stop seeing all of them, so she could concentrate on her job. She tried to look over the boy's shoulder when she came round to sweep by the windows. He didn't notice – he was far too interested in the book. Even the cat appeared to be reading it. Rose crept closer, and discovered to her disappointment that Freddie was not reading the spellbook. He had a comic tucked inside the pages, and was deep in the adventures of *Jack Jones, Hero of the Seven Seas*. Jack Jones was currently struggling with a giant squid. Rose sighed disgustedly, right behind Freddie, and he shut the book at once with a guilty snap. Rose ignored him. Briskly, she swept up her dust-pile and made for the door. Perhaps tomorrow, when she was dusting, she could sneak a look at *Prendergast's Perfect Primer*.

As she left, the white cat and the white boy were still watching her, with narrow eyes.

FIVE

After Rose had cleaned the workroom, she went down the stairs backwards to see if it would confuse whatever the magic in them was, but it didn't. Rose was sure she could hear the house giggling – but it seemed a friendly sort of noise, not a nasty sniggering one. All the same, she stubbornly stayed backwards all the way down to the kitchen, and it was tricky, especially as she was carrying the brush and the dustpan too. Turning the corner of the first-floor staircase – the last one before she got to the back stairs, which she was sure would be safe – Rose gleefully went too fast, and one foot slipped out from under her on the deep carpet, and got hooked in the sweeping brush somehow, and she went tumbling and bouncing down the steps. Rose squeaked with horror, thinking all at once of Mr Freddie and the Ming vase, and being sent back to the orphanage in disgrace. However oddly magical the Fountain house was, she wasn't going back – never, never, never! The house seemed to approve. As she thought it, defiantly, tears springing to her eyes, something caught her, and set her back on her feet.

Something. Someone? Something with strong arms. Furry ones. Rose gulped, and sat down on the deep red-patterned carpet of the sixth step, and looked up cautiously at the stuffed bear in the deep embrasure in the wall. Its glass eyes stared off into the distance, and its paws were innocently folded on its fat, rather balding tummy. The gaslight shone on its enormous hooked black claws, but its face was foolish and not fierce. *Who, me?* she imagined it asking. *I'm stuffed, dear. Can't move, me. No, you caught the banisters, that's all. You be careful now, pet.*

But something was chuckling, just beyond her hearing, as she crept down the last few steps.

That's it, dear. You go forwards, this time. Safer that way, see?

Rose crept into the kitchen, trying not to hear the bear's voice whispering in her ears, and trying to look as though the house was just a large and boring place she had to clean, and not a mass of twisting staircases and talking furniture that scared and fascinated her at the same time.

'I've finished, Miss,' she told Miss Bridges, trying to look bright and keen and not like a person who talked to bears. Or rather, a person that bears talked to. That was what made it so unfair. She'd never talked to a bear in her life. She'd never asked to talk to bears!

Behind Miss Bridges, Bill sat at the table, his hair more like a doormat than ever. He was eating a huge slice of bread and dripping, but he still managed to smirk round it, and simper, in a way that made it quite clear he thought Rose was sucking up. She shot him a *Just you wait* look. Somehow the knowledge that he was from St Bartholomew's made him feel almost brotherly. In the sense that she could imagine pulling his hair (if it weren't so short) or stealing his sweets.

'Good girl,' Miss Bridges said approvingly. And without even glancing round, she added, 'And you, Bill, stop pulling faces. The master's boots aren't done yet. Off you go.'

Rose was very impressed. She eyed Miss Bridges cautiously. She'd been fairly sure that the orphanage story about Miss Lockwood's glass eye had been false, but in this house, she wasn't so sure. She wouldn't put it past Miss Bridges to have something clever concealed in that smooth knot of hair at the back of her neck.

'Common sense, Rose, that's all.' Miss Bridges sounded amused. 'I've never known Bill not to be pulling faces. Come along, dear, work to do.' And she sailed off, her black frock rustling importantly, with Rose pattering after her.

Miss Bridges was what the girls at the orphanage would probably have called a right tartar, but all that really meant was that she liked things to be done properly, and she didn't like to see people sitting about doing nothing. As the housekeeper, Miss Bridges had her own room, along the corridor from the kitchen. It was a sort of sitting room, but there was a desk too, for her to do the household accounts, and write the orders for the tradesmen. There was also an enormous cupboard, full of odds and ends and treasures. Rose's new boots had come out of it – nice black buttoned ones which had belonged to some maidservant long ago, but which fitted Rose so well that she kept wriggling her toes in admiration. Miss Bridges went to it now, and burrowed about at the back, emerging at last with a small basket, neatly lined in blue gingham. 'Here you are, Rose. I don't like my maids to be idle, so when you've a spare moment, you can be at some mending.'

Rose gazed at it speechlessly. A needle case – just a scrap of felt, to be sure, but with two bright needles in it. A spool of black darning wool, and a battered thimble, and her own darning mushroom! Her eyes pricked with tears at such richness.

'Though do remember, Rose,' Miss Bridges reminded her sternly, 'that although you may do your sewing in the kitchen, you must darn your stockings in the privacy of your own room. It would never do to let Bill or, heaven forbid, the butcher's boy, catch a glimpse of your stockings.'

Rose shook her head, appalled at the very idea. 'I shan't, Miss,' she promised fervently.

'Good. Now, I have some errands for you to run, and I should think Mrs Jones will have some things for you to get as well.'

'You mean, shopping, Miss? On my own?'

Miss Bridges nodded. 'Running errands is an important part of your job, Rose. Don't worry, you'll have a list, and directions.' A tiny frown creased her forehead for a moment. 'Rose, you can read?'

Rose tried not to sound indignant. 'Of course, Miss! They were very enlightened, at the orphanage. I can write, too.'

'Good. Good.' Miss Bridges started to write on a scrap of paper, in elegant sloping handwriting. 'Now, most of the housekeeping supplies are sent over by the shops, of course, but there are the odd things.

I need some more silver polish for a start, as we seem to have almost run out.'

Rose tried not to look guilty. She and Bill had been rather lavish with it the day before.

Mrs Jones was drinking her mid-morning tea, reading her newspaper, and tutting. 'Little boy gone missing from right outside his house, Miss Bridges, isn't that sad? Mind you, it'll be the parents' fault. People should take better care, that's what I say. And another revolution in one of them Far Eastern places. I don't know what the world's coming to, I'm sure I don't.'

'Quite.' Miss Bridges indicated her list. 'Do you have any commissions for Rose, Mrs Jones?'

Mrs Jones brightened immediately. 'Oh, now, let me see. Yes, if Rose is going to the grocer's, Miss Bridges, I need some more of those crystallised violets. You know how partial Miss Isabella is to those, and they're quite gone.' She added to Miss Bridges' list with a pencil stub from her apron pocket. 'And she could go to the fishmonger's about that crab. They're only round the corner. She can give them this note. I will not be fobbed off with that mingy little specimen. Crab, indeed. A fat spider, that's what it was.' She scribbled industriously. 'You will be careful, won't you, Rose dear? You're not used to those busy streets. You find a policeman, and get him to help you cross. You'd better draw her a map, Miss Bridges, you've more of a sense for directions than I have.' She looked up, and sucked the end of her pencil thoughtfully. 'Or better yet, send Bill with her the first time she's out, don't you think?'

Miss Bridges looked doubtful. 'Perhaps.'

Bill appeared at the door from the back kitchen, looking innocent, and with a smear of boot polish on his nose. 'Did you want me, Miss?'

Miss Bridges eyed him consideringly. 'Very well. You can accompany Rose, but you're to take her straight to the fishmonger's, no dawdling about with those unsuitable friends of yours. Go and put your proper livery on. And Rose, fetch your cloak.'

Rose had no idea what Miss Bridges was talking about, but when Bill came back two minutes later, she discovered that livery meant a black jacket with greeny-gold frogging all across the front, and a rather odd-shaped hat.

'Don't you dare laugh,' Bill hissed in her ear, as they endured another set of instructions from Mrs Jones. Miss Bridges had gone back to her room, to write a sternly worded letter to the chimney sweep about the presence of a bird's nest in the drawing-room chimney.

Mrs Jones bustled about, finding Rose a basket, and telling them to put the polish and the violets on the

Fountain account at the grocer. Then she looked a little cautiously out of the kitchen towards Miss Bridges' door, and handed them each a penny from the knitted purse she kept in one of the jelly moulds. 'Buy yourself some bull's-eyes, Rose, or something nice. Bill, you are not to buy that horrid pink sherbet stuff. I will not have you being sick all over my kitchen like you were last time I gave you money for sweets.'

Bill shook his head, as if sherbet was the furthest thing from his mind. 'Come on then,' he told Rose, bowing her out onto the area steps as though she was a duchess.

Rose stalked past him with her nose in the air, trying not to giggle. 'Which way do we go?' she asked him eagerly, as the area gate clanged to behind them. It sent a shudder of delicious excitement running down Rose's spine. They were off out on their own, and she even had a penny to spend!

Bill gave her a superior look. 'This way, mouse, and don't you show me up.'

'Don't need to,' Rose retorted. 'Have you seen what that hat looks like?'

Bill flushed. 'Miss Bridges thinks it's smart,' he muttered. 'I look like I've got a flowerpot on me head.'

'It isn't really that bad,' Rose promised him, feeling guilty. 'And at least it fits.'

'I suppose. Come on. We got to get to the fishmonger, and that's down this way.'

Rose followed, trying to remember the route, but Bill took so many alleyways and cut-throughs that she was quite lost by the time they fetched up in the middle of a busy street, packed with people and carriages. Rose stopped at the end of the alley, lifting her skirt away from a pile of rubbish, and looking panicked.

'What's up?' Bill turned back impatiently as he realised she wasn't following.

'There's so many of them!' Rose whispered.

Bill looked out at the street again, as though he was seeing it differently. 'Yeah. I suppose there is. I forgot what it's like, coming from the orphanage.' He blinked, and Rose could see him thinking back. Then he gave himself a little shake. 'Don't worry, Rosie, no one'll hurt you. Mind you don't get pushed in the road though, some of them horses goes awful quick.'

Rose nodded. The horses were enormous shiny beasts, stamping and snorting with flaring red nostrils. The carriages were mostly open ones, with ladies in them, bowing and smiling to acquaintances as they passed.

'Does Mr Fountain have a carriage and horses like that?' she murmured to Bill.

'Course. He's got a barouche, like that one over there.

And two black horses. He keeps them in the mews, round the back. The groom and the coachman come in for their meals some of the time, but mostly Mrs Jones sends me round the stable with a basket for them. Miss Bridges thinks stable company is low.'

Rose nodded, and tried to look as though she knew what he was talking about. It didn't work. Bill just grinned at her pityingly. 'You'll pick it up. Hey! Mind, you!'

Rose felt a tug on her skirt, and squeaked in dismay, pulling back and huddling herself close to Bill. The pile of raggedy rubbish she'd been standing next to had turned into a child, who'd been sleeping against the wall, wrapped in a dirty cloak.

Bill hustled her away into the street, muttering crossly about cheek, but Rose looked back in horror at the child's pinched cheeks. 'Got a penny, Miss, just a penny, for some food?' she heard it calling after her. She couldn't tell if it had been a boy or a girl.

'Shouldn't we go back?' she asked Bill worriedly.

Bill looked at her in amazement. 'What on earth for?'

'She – I mean, he – that child only wanted a penny. And I've got one!' Rose gazed back, but the child had subsided back into the alley, she could see one bare grey foot just sticking out round the wall. She shivered. It could have been her. All those improving stories the orphanage schoolmistress had read them, where children died of cold in the street – she'd known they were true, and felt grateful, but she'd never quite been able to imagine it. After all, she had never been outside the orphanage. Now suddenly Rose saw that they were all too real. She *had* been lucky.

'Bill, please?' she begged, but he was already heading off up the street, impatient with her, and she had to run to catch him up. She didn't dare let him out of her sight.

'You're soft, Rose,' he told her, as he felt her apologetic tug on his gold-braided sleeve. 'You'll learn. Beggars are everywhere, you can't give to them all.'

'I suppose,' she agreed sadly. 'It was just that it was a penny, and that's what I had.'

Bill sniffed, then he halted his step for a second, stood up straighter and started to walk faster, Rose still scuttling after him.

'What is it?' she asked anxiously.

Another boy was walking towards them, in a similar livery jacket to Bill's, except his was green, and he hadn't been afflicted with a stovepipe hat. Instead he had a velvet cap with far too many rows of gold braid.

Rose could feel Bill bristling like a dog, and the other boy was eyeing them watchfully.

'Nursemaiding, are we?' the other boy sneered,

jerking his thumb at Rose.

Rose tried to hide behind Bill, and Bill tried to look as though he didn't know she was there. They nearly tripped over each other. Bill glared at Rose, and the other boy sniggered.

'New housemaid,' Bill mumbled. Then he decided to go on the attack. 'What you got a pancake on your head for?' he demanded.

'You can talk. Could use you for skittles with that thing on.'

The two boys watched each other suspiciously for a second or two, before they reckoned enough insults had been exchanged.

'All right then?' Bill muttered. 'Rose, this is George. He's from St Bartholomew's too. Got a job in a smart house over the other side of the park now. She's from St Bridget's,' he explained to George.

'You know my sister, Eliza? She all right?' George asked.

Rose nodded shyly. She could see the likeness now. He was covered in freckles, just like Eliza. She didn't like to say that she'd done Liza out of a job.

'Liza's fine,' she whispered.

George nodded. He probably hadn't seen Eliza for years except in church, Rose thought with surprise, even though they'd lived next door to each other.

'You seen Jack?' he asked Bill now, frowning a little.

Bill shook his head. 'Not for a couple of weeks. Why?'

George folded his arms and hissed dramatically, 'Disappeared!'

'What?' Bill sounded scornful.

'Gone. Vamoosed. Done a runner!'

'Why would he do that? And where's he gone to, anyway? Load of nonsense,' Bill scoffed.

'S'true though. Didn't go home one day. The coachman from his place came round to ask me if I knew where he was, 'cause he knew I was from the same orphanage. Jack's just gone.'

'Run off to join the circus probably,' Bill chuckled. 'He was always mad on it. Bareback riding. He'll be back in a while.' He frowned. 'He's stupid though. They won't take him on again. He'll get sent back to the orphanage.'

George shook his head. 'Nope. They won't have him. He'll be in the workhouse, for sure. Anyway. Gotta get back. Be seeing you.'

He strolled on, and Bill led Rose further up the street, his expression grim. 'Can't believe he'd do that,' he said quietly. 'Stupid, that's what it is.'

'Was he a friend of yours?' Rose asked him shyly.

'Yeah. We all left St Bartholomew's at the same time. Jack's a couple of years younger though. And he was only there a short while, his dad went off to fight in the war, and never came back. Then his mum got a fever and passed on. So he turned up with us. Always said he shouldn't be there, he wasn't an orphan, and his dad was coming back for him. Not gonna happen though.' Bill shook his head. 'He was a stableboy at a house near George's place. Always loved horses. He was happy, an' all! Why'd he go off without saying anything?'

'Is this the fishmonger's?' Rose asked, grabbing Bill's coat as he walked on, staring at the pavement. She'd spotted a sign with a painted fish on it, swinging above their heads.

'What? Oh! Yeah. Come on then.' Bill led her into the tiled doorway and through the smart glass door, and Rose gazed round at the piled counters. They'd always had fish on Friday at the orphanage, but it was horrible. The cheapest fish the cook could find, and it stank. Small wonder she hated fish, even without her added history. There was a faint fishy whiff in here, but nothing like the orphanage kitchen on a Friday morning. And the fish – they were like monsters! Rose had never imagined fish could be so big – one of them was half as big as her. They were laid out on marble slabs, with chunks of ice and tufts of green stuff decorating them. Their eyes seemed to roll and follow Rose as she approached the counter, a mass of silvery scales. Greenish black clawed things were piled up on one side, looking more like the sort of thing Rose had expected to see in the workroom back at the house – disgusting spell ingredients. She peered at them, intrigued, and then jumped back with a tiny scream when one of them waved a claw at her. They were alive!

Someone sniggered from behind the counter, and Rose flushed, looking up at a boy a little older than Bill, wrapped in an enormous blue and white striped apron.

'You shut up,' Bill told him in a lordly fashion. 'We're here to complain, see. Rose, give that overgrown beanpole the note.'

Rose drew it out of her basket and passed it over the counter. Despite the shining marble slabs, the boy's fingernails were grubby and encrusted with shiny scales. She wrinkled her nose disapprovingly.

The boy read it, slowly. 'That were a perfectly good crab!' he muttered. 'Old skinflint. Me dad's out the back taking the delivery in, I'll give it to him later. You'd better have one on account, anyway. Here.' He reached over to the pile of clawed monsters and grabbed one. 'This do for her?'

The crab wriggled a claw feebly – its pincers were tied closed with string – and Rose shrank back in horror.

'Well, come on!' the boy snapped. 'What, you want

a bigger one? She don't ask much, does she? All right then.' He dug around in the heaving pile, and eventually brought out an enormous crab, waving it in Rose's face. 'Will this do, then?'

Rose nodded. The crab glared at her from fierce little black eyes, and attempted to clack its claws. Its back legs waved madly, and Rose gulped. It was like a spider, only much, *much* bigger.

'Can you – wrap it up?' she stammered. She simply couldn't walk home with it in her basket just like that. It looked like it would climb out and start eating people.

The boy heaved a sigh, and started to swathe the creature in paper. Eventually he held out a wriggling parcel, and Rose held the basket up to the counter. Even through the paper, she wasn't touching that thing. She wasn't squeamish about mice, at all – no one who'd lived at St Bridget's could be – they were everywhere. She'd even woken up once to find a rat sitting on her bedcover, eyeing her as though he thought she might be tasty. She hadn't screamed. She'd flung a boot at him, and he'd scuttled off. All the girls knew to make sure their toes were well tucked inside their blankets if they wanted them to still be there in the morning. But Rose had a horror of things with too many legs. Anything with over five, and she didn't want it anywhere near her. The crab was like the worst spider she'd ever seen, and then about seventeen of its friends, all rolled into one. It was squirming in her basket now.

Rose looked hopefully at Bill as she followed him out of the shop, leaving the fishmonger's boy muttering irritably.

'Not a chance,' he told her, smirking. 'I'm not going round carrying a basket like that. I'd look a proper mooncalf. Come on, let's do the rest of the shopping. You can put the silver polish on top of the crab, and then it won't wriggle so much.'

Rose followed him, holding the basket away from her as much as possible, and trying not to look at it.

The grocer's was an unbelievable treasure house. Rose had already been shocked by the amount of food that was eaten at the Fountain house – not just the amazing dishes that Mrs Jones concocted for Mr Fountain's dinners, but the meals she was served in the kitchen, mostly cooked by Sarah the kitchen maid. Meat every day! Sometimes twice! And cups of tea, and odd bits of cake. Not to mention the huge slabs of bread and dripping that Bill seemed to be tucking into whenever she saw him. Not that they made him any the less skinny. Rose supposed that he was making up for all his years of never-quite-enough at the orphanage.

But this shop was packed with food. Great, towering

piles of it. Sacks overflowing, tins tottering, enormous hams swinging from beams up above. A flock of small boys swarmed up and down spindly ladders fetching the produce from the ranks of shelves. It was like a temple dedicated to eating. Rose couldn't help feeling that it was all rather improper. Still, at least the tin of silver polish and the packet of crystallised violets hid the crab a little bit.

Bill pulled his penny out of his trouser pocket, and led Rose over to a small counter in front of a sparkling array of glass jars filled with brightly coloured sweets. A pretty girl in a frilled white apron turned to serve them. At least, she was pretty until she smiled, and then Rose couldn't tear her eyes away from the girl's teeth – her mouth was filled with blackened stumps.

Bill didn't seem to notice. 'Pennyworth of sherbet, please!' he said eagerly.

'Mrs Jones said you weren't to have that!' Rose reminded him, banging the basket into his leg. He glared at her, and added, 'The green kind! All right, Little Miss Know-it-all?'

'You'll still be sick, I bet,' Rose muttered, but he ignored her.

'Would you like anything, Miss?' the shop girl asked. Rose tried not to stare at her teeth, and looked at the rows of jars instead. She had no idea.

'Butterscotch?' the girl suggested. 'Liquorice pipes? A sherbet fountain? Toffee? Aniseed balls?'

'Not those, Rose, you wouldn't like them, they're disgusting,' Bill told her firmly.

Rose was almost wishing she didn't have a penny. The girl was starting to look irritable, and Bill wouldn't stop laughing at her. 'What are those?' she asked desperately, pointing to one of the jars.

'These?' The shop girl lifted down a jar, and Rose gasped with delight. She'd pointed at random, but they were so pretty. Little pillow-shaped sweets in glorious stripes – pink and white, green and gold, purple and red. They looked like something from a fairy tale; Rose could see a princess's bed piled with them.

'What are they called?' she asked, thinking that they'd probably be something dismal like cough drops.

'Chocolate satins. Want them?'

'Oh, yes!' Rose nodded eagerly, watching as the jewel-like sweets poured into a paper bag. The name was perfect, too. It was like being handed treasure. She gave her penny over the counter, with a tiny pang of doubt, remembering the beggar-child. It didn't feel fair – but these were her first ever sweets. Didn't she deserve them?

They strolled along the street, Bill dipping his finger in the sherbet bag blissfully, until his black livery was covered in a faint dusting of green, and Rose cautiously sucking a chocolate satin – the green and gold kind, which reminded her of the frog prince in the one book of fairy tales in the schoolroom at St Bridget's.

'Oh, they're different in the middle!' she exclaimed after a while.

'That's the *chocolate*, Rose!' Bill sighed. 'Chocolate satins? Honestly.'

But Rose wasn't listening. She was some way behind him, staring silently into another plate-glass window. Bill found himself telling empty air how she was that dumb she was asking to be stolen by slave traders. He turned round and pelted back.

'What are you doing? I nearly lost you! Come on! I'm never going anywhere with you again, it's like herding a cat.'

Rose seemed to be stuck to the floor. Really stuck, for when he tugged her, all she did was lean slightly. He couldn't shift her at all.

'Look!' she whispered, enthralled. She was pointing at something in the window. Dresses, Bill supposed at a guess, but when he looked too, he saw it was a toy shop. An enormous doll, dressed in a white fur cloak, was staring grandly out at them. She had golden hair in ringlets – real hair, Bill thought. His mother had sold her hair once, but she hadn't got much, because it was only brown, not a fashionable auburn. He remembered being horrified to see her with short spikes all over her head, like a boy. Beside the doll stood a perfectly miniature little dog, a curly white French poodle on a blue leather lead that the doll held in her kidgloved hand. She was surrounded by doll's furniture, including a little gold-painted wardrobe, out of which spilled more silk and lace outfits.

'Suppose you've never seen a doll,' Bill suggested. 'Big one, isn't it?'

'I have,' Rose murmured. 'Miss Isabella has one almost as big. But this one moved!' She glanced up at him, pleadingly. 'Really it did, Bill, I'm not lying. She waved to me! Is it magic?' She turned back, and then clutched his arm. 'Oh, look! Look!'

Again the doll stiffly raised one arm in a grand lady's regal wave, and this time the little white dog barked too, in a strangely squeaky voice.

Bill looked at it carefully, then peered round the side of the doll, pressing his nose to the window. 'Nah. Thought so. Clockwork. Look, Rose, you can see the key.'

Rose leaned in to see too. He was right. Sticking out of the doll's back was a large silver key. As they watched, the doll's mouth opened slightly, and she said 'Ma-ma!' before the key clicked round.

'You wind her up, and she does all those things one after the other,' Bill explained. 'Clever.'

Rose stared at the doll, disappointed. 'I thought it was a spell,' she said sadly. She'd imagined a magic doll, who could sit at the little tea table in the window next to her, and drink from the flower-painted china, like a tiny girl.

Bill snorted. 'Doll fit for a princess, that would be. That thing probably costs ten years' wages as it is. If it had a spell on, you'd be paying it off for a century!' He looked down at her, frowning. 'What do you think magic's for, Rose? It doesn't get wasted on dolls. Too expensive. Too *rare*. Don't go thinking it's all over the place, just because Mr Fountain can click his fingers and it rains rose petals.'

'Can he?' Rose asked excitedly.

'Only if someone's paying him a king's ransom for it. Magic's serious stuff.' Bill frowned at her.

Rose nodded. She understood what Bill was saying, but she just couldn't bring herself to believe it. There was so much richness here in the world outside St Bridget's. And however important and special magic was, she'd only seen it telling stories on shiny things. That wasn't serious at all. Surely magic couldn't be all to do with making gold? That seemed so sad.

'Look, if magic was easy to get, do you think we'd be

polishing the silver all the time? It'd have spells on it to keep it shiny instead. And there'd be self-lighting fires, and plates that washed themselves.' Bill shook his head. 'People are cheaper, Rose. We're cheaper.'

'So you don't ever see it, then?' Rose asked sadly. 'There's never magic things in shops, or anything like that?'

Bill shrugged. 'Oh, sometimes, maybe. The odd one. But only basic stuff. The kind of thing Mr Fountain does, no shop could afford it.'

Rose grasped at the thread of hope. She hadn't seen much magic at the house yet – it was all hidden away in the workroom, and she only went in there to clean – and she couldn't help being fascinated by it. She'd never seen anything magical, apart from her strange pictures. She was hoping they'd stopped now, but she would love to see some real magic. Maybe even touch it. *What did magic feel like?* she wondered, idling down the street after Bill. Like sparks, running over her fingers...or perhaps like trying to walk through a puddle of treacle... Rose frowned. Treacle? Where had that come from?

'Oy! Rose! Watch that horse!'

Rose whirled round in horror, realising that she had accidentally strayed too close to the edge of the pavement, and now an enormous white horse was bearing down on her, ridden by a gentleman in an even taller hat than Bill's.

'Out of the way, girl!' the man shouted, cutting at her with his whip.

Rose cried out as it hit her across the face. She dropped the basket, and Bill hauled her away, cursing. Rose was vaguely aware of being quite impressed. He knew a lot of words.

Then she realised that not all of them were coming from Bill. The man who had hit her was still yelling, because he was covered in treacle.

'Did you do that?' Bill whispered, staring.

'I don't know!' Rose assured him. 'Not on purpose!' Her face burned, but she couldn't help smiling. The horse was gazing at her helplessly, treacle dripping down its long white nose. It looked particularly foolish.

'Was this you, girl? Did you throw this stuff at me?' The man was leaning down out of the saddle now, reaching to grab her, and Rose squeaked in dismay.

'Come on!' Bill grabbed the basket – the paper-wrapped crab had been trying to make a getaway, and one claw was sticking out of the parcel – and dragged Rose down an alley.

'Where does this go?' Rose gasped as they raced along.

'No idea!' Bill panted. 'Away from him! Honestly, Rose, I knew there was something odd about you, but

I didn't think you were one of *them*.'

'I'm not!' Rose wailed. 'I don't know anything about magic, stuff just happens to me!'

Bill slowed down, looking behind them anxiously.

'I don't think he followed us.' He sniggered, almost reluctantly. 'He looked like a swamp monster from the Black Lagoon.'

Rose gave him a sharp look. It sounded as though Bill and Freddie had the same taste in comics, despite being as different as they possibly could be in everything else.

'I really don't do it on purpose,' she pleaded. 'Maybe I'm cursed? It doesn't happen very often,' she promised him earnestly.

Bill sniffed. 'It'd better not. You'll get in a sight of trouble if it does.' He grabbed her chin, and turned her face this way and that. 'He didn't mark you, then?' he muttered, and Rose realised gratefully that he hadn't wanted her to be hurt, even if she was a strange one.

They walked silently back to the house, Bill giving her worried, almost resentful looks every so often. Rose felt no desire to look about her at the beautiful houses and grand squares they were passing. All she could think was that it was just as she had feared. Bill had found out what she was like, and now he hated her. He'd called her *one of them*. She didn't want to be one

83

of them! He thought she was like Mr Freddie, that stuck-up white mouse of a boy. And Miss Isabella, a horrid, spoilt little princess, who kept the house in an uproar with her tantrums and demands. Rose wasn't like that! As soon as she possibly could, Rose resolved, she was going to get into the workroom and read that Prendergast book. Then she'd be able to get rid of this stupid magic, and stop it ruining her lovely new life.

Mrs Jones received the crab with approval, and gratefully accepted a chocolate satin, saying she'd always had a fancy for them. She drove Bill out into the yard, and swiped the sherbert from his jacket with a clothes brush while he was still in it, but he wasn't sick this time. And moaning about being beaten up distracted Bill from what Rose had done for a little while. At least, he didn't mention it to anyone, but for the rest of the day, Rose kept catching him eyeing her in a thoughtful sort of way. She took to making rude faces back. It was the most unmagical thing she could think of to do.

SIX

Miss Bridges bustled into the back kitchen looking slightly harassed. Rose blinked at her. Mrs Jones looked harassed all the time, especially when Bill was anywhere near, but Miss Bridges was usually serenely calm.

'Ah, Rose.' Miss Bridges managed a regal smile, and Rose hurriedly put down the crystal drop she was polishing. Miss Bridges had announced that morning that now they had Rose to help, they really ought to take down the chandelier and clean it, as it was looking decidedly grubby. Everyone had congregated in the main hallway, the grandest part of the house, watching Bill wobble on a stepladder. Rose couldn't help thinking that this was one of those jobs that a spell would make so much easier. Bill had been standing on tiptoe at the very top of the ladder, swaying sickeningly. Rose had closed her eyes – she simply couldn't watch any more in case it all came crashing down on top of him.

'Is he all right?' she whispered to Susan. 'He's not going to fall, is he?'

Susan gave a disgusted little snort. 'What are you worrying about that grubby little toad for? You're sweet on him, aren't you!'

Rose's eyes flew open. 'I am not!' she snapped. 'I just don't want him to fall off that ladder. If he brings the chandelier down it'll be me sweeping it up, won't it?' It hadn't taken her long to realise that Susan had an amazing talent for being somewhere else when the nasty jobs needed doing.

Susan only smirked, as Miss Bridges was eyeing them, but as soon as the housekeeper turned round to call more directions to Bill, she gave Rose's arm a vicious pinch. 'Show a bit of respect for your elders and betters, Miss!'

Rose hissed with pain, and mentally added to her revenge list for Susan. She'd seen some quite impressive tricks at the orphanage, but she wanted to be settled in her job for a little longer before she did anything risky. Let her just wait… A yelp from Bill made her dig her fingernails into her palms. 'Please don't let him fall!' she whispered to she-didn't-know-who.

'Oh!' Susan sounded surprised, and rather disappointed, and Rose opened her eyes, too anxious not to see what was happening. There hadn't been a crash; surely that was a good sign?

Bill was standing at the bottom of the ladder, trailing an armful of crystals and looking relieved, if somewhat confused. 'It was a lot lighter than it looked,' he muttered.

Rose blinked. She looked at the chandelier, sparkling innocently in the sunlit hallway. It seemed to send little motes of light bouncing and glittering round the marble pillars, so that the whole room glimmered. The effect was – magical.

Rose stared hard at the chandelier. She couldn't tell. It might just have been good luck. Or maybe not. She glanced over her shoulder and shivered as the servants went in procession down the back stairs to the kitchens.

Was it her imagination, or, as the great hallway emptied out, could she hear the house breathing?

Rose looked up at Miss Bridges. 'Did you want me, Miss?' she asked anxiously, wondering if she'd done something wrong. It would be good if the Fountain house had Rules, like the ones at the orphanage. Rules that got read out every week, so everyone knew what was expected of them.

'Mr Fountain has a moment to see you, Rose,' Miss

Bridges announced, in a voice that made Rose feel this was a royal command.

She looked helplessly at the brown apron she was wearing.

'No, no, the new white one, Rose, here,' Miss Bridges frowned. 'Quickly!'

Rose flurried into the new apron – the first time she'd worn it. It wasn't as fancy as Susan's – Rose coveted Susan's frills in a way she knew was quite sinful – but it was crisply starched and it had a large bow at the back, which she couldn't help craning her neck to admire.

Miss Bridges surveyed her critically, and twitched the bow straight. 'You'll do. Come along then, we mustn't keep the master waiting.'

'Would he be angry?' Rose asked anxiously, as she jogged after Miss Bridges. Even while she worried, a little bit of Rose couldn't help speculating whether the housekeeper had wheels instead of legs under that black frock. She moved so fast, in a sort of polite glide.

Miss Bridges smiled over her shoulder, gliding onwards. 'No, not at all, Rose. But he's very busy. I happened to catch him at the right moment, and mentioned your arrival. If we leave it too long, he – well, he might not be paying attention any more...' Miss Bridges sighed. 'He's a *very* important man, Rose.'

Mr Fountain's study was one of the grander rooms, the ones that Susan cleaned, so Rose hadn't seen it before. She didn't see much of it now, except to notice that it had a very beautiful carpet, a woven one, full of animals and birds and strange creatures that might have been both.

'And this is…er…' A deep, purring voice wrapped itself round Rose's ears, making her jump nervously.

'Rose, Sir,' Miss Bridges reminded him, pushing Rose forwards firmly. 'The little girl from St Bridget's. She's been with us two days, and I'm sure she'll settle in very nicely.' She eyed Rose expectantly, and Rose bobbed a curtsey, and said quietly, 'Very pleased I'm sure, Sir.' She wasn't quite sure what she was supposed to say, and it seemed to cover all the eventualities.

Mr Fountain leaned towards her over an enormous expanse of black marble-topped desk, which had several strange brass instruments ticking and swinging on it. The desk looked like an expensive gravestone, Rose thought nervously, fixing her eyes on the silvery threads running through it.

'You're quite right.' The voice had lost some of its purr now, and was sharper. Interested, instead of polite. 'I often think so myself. It belonged to my first teacher, and I'm afraid he was a terrible show-off.'

Rose glanced up at him shyly, feeling quite sure that

she had only *thought* about the gravestone. Mr Fountain drooped one eyelid in the ghost of a wink. Miss Bridges didn't appear to have noticed. She was looking at a dusty ornament with an expression that did not bode well for Susan.

'Isn't it cold to write on?' Rose asked, forgetting to be polite and putting a finger on the black marble. Then she jumped back in surprise. 'Oh! It burned me!'

'Like I said, a terrible show-off,' said Mr Fountain. 'He enchanted it, in case of espionage. Spying, my dear. A dreadful curse in the new magical society. Stealing of spells is rife. Only the owner of this desk can touch it, you see, and it has to be magically willed to its next owner on one's deathbed. An awful bore, as I can't get rid of the thing. I shall probably leave it to Freddie.'

Rose eyed the marble cautiously, and then looked up at her master for the first time. His moustache was unnetted now, and swooped out to his ears in a glossy brown curl. It looked ridiculous, but his eyes were bright and curious above it. 'However does Susan dust it?' she asked.

Mr Fountain blinked. 'I don't think she does,' he murmured. 'I hadn't thought about that. I waft my handkerchief over it occasionally.'

'It is awfully dusty,' Rose pointed out. She heard Miss Bridges' sharp intake of breath, and realised that even without Rules, she ought to have known not to tell off her master about the state of his desk. Still, it was quite true. She bobbed another curtsey, and Miss Bridges shooed her to the door.

'I shall keep an eye on you, young Rose,' Mr Fountain's voice followed her. He was purring again, and as Rose looked back, she saw that he had his feet up on the enchanted marble.

After that, Rose wished she could be the one to clean the study. She was sure she would do it better than Susan – it hadn't only been the desk that was dusty, she'd noted. She wanted to look at all those strange instruments, and study the carpet a little more. And brush it, to get those muddy footprints out. If she used a feather duster, she might even be able to get the desk clean. Or would the spell sizzle the feathers? Honestly, she didn't think magic was as clever and wonderful as all that, if no one ever considered the dusting. She sighed. Maybe dusting was just too boring and unimportant to think about. Then Rose frowned to herself. What if dust got in the way? What if a magician was doing a spell, and enchanted the dust by mistake? If the spell from Mr Fountain's desk had landed on dust instead, it would go floating through the air, looking for its owner, and burning things! What if it landed on someone's skin? Rose shuddered. That wouldn't happen. Would it? Uneasily, she remembered Mr Freddie flying down the stairs and breaking a Ming vase. Enchanted dust didn't actually sound all that unlikely. She resolved to be extremely careful of piles of dust from now on.

Anyway, cleaning Mr Fountain's private study was strictly the senior housemaid's job. Even though Susan didn't work very hard, she would jump on Rose if she suggested taking over any of her duties – she would prefer to bully Rose into doing them, and then take the credit, whilst looking smugly angelic.

'Gloves! Rose! Yes, good girl, make sure you keep them clean. *William Sands, where are your gloves?!*'

'Dunno, Miss.' Bill stared at Miss Bridges with the expression of a particularly stupid mule. Rose knew him well enough after nearly a week to know that it was put on. Bill knew perfectly well where his gloves were, she was sure. He just enjoyed baiting Miss Bridges.

'They're in his pockets,' Susan said in a saintly voice. She was wearing a very smart black coat that Rose guessed she must have saved her wages for, and a little black bonnet with a bunch of velvet violets on it. Rose was quite ashamed to realise how pleased she was that the violets made Susan look sallow. But not so ashamed that she intended to stop thinking it.

'Put them on!' Miss Bridges hissed. 'This household must be well turned out for church. I will not have slovenliness.'

'She has a competition with Mrs Lark across the road,' the kitchen maid, Sarah, whispered in Rose's ear, seeing her amazed expression. 'Not that she'd ever admit it.'

'Oh!' Rose breathed. That explained it. She'd never seen Miss Bridges so het up.

As they hurried up the area steps to wait for the family to come out of the front door, Rose saw another, very similar party forming up across the square. A fat little lady in a purple mantle was cuffing the ear of a boy in a livery even fancier than Bill's. The jacket had tails, and it appeared he'd had a comic concealed in a secret tailpocket.

Miss Bridges permitted herself a small, very gracious smile as she lifted a hand in a wave. Mrs Lark pretended not to see.

'I bloomin' well hope it's a short sermon today,' Bill said, tugging on his hated gloves. 'Nearly fell asleep last Sunday.'

Sarah shrugged. 'Why don't you just watch the glass? That's what I do. It's quite fun.'

Rose looked at them uncertainly. Watch the glass? Did the vicar have an hourglass for his sermon? She glanced at Sarah. She'd been nice to Rose, so much so that Rose occasionally wished that she was a kitchen maid, too. But Sarah seemed to spend all her time at the scullery sink, with mountains of washing-up. Her hands were cracked and scarlet from the hot water, and she almost never left the kitchens. No, even with Susan to put up with, housemaiding was better than that. But Rose was strangely disappointed. How could Sarah enjoy watching an hourglass? It was just – sand. Trickling through a hole. Maybe she just liked not watching water and pans.

At that moment the front door swung open, and Mr Fountain strolled down the steps in a very shiny top hat. He was followed by Freddie and Isabella; Freddie in a black velvet suit with a lace collar, and Isabella in a white lace dress, and a little white fur jacket. She looked remarkably like the doll Rose had seen in the toy shop.

'Oh no,' Susan muttered. 'I hate that dress. It's a pig to iron. She *would* choose that one. And I'll have to starch Freddie's collar, Mrs Trump's useless at starching.'

Bill sniggered, and Susan eyed him sharply. 'You watch it. Miss Bridges loves lace. I bet she'd think a gold lace collar would really add to your Sunday livery. You'd be well up on Ernest across the road in one of those. Perhaps I should suggest it,' she said sweetly, staring at the sky.

'You wouldn't!' Bill breathed in horror.

'I know who left that dead mouse in the dining room cutlery drawer!' Susan spat, and Bill tried hard to look innocent, but couldn't stop himself sputtering with laughter.

The church looked more like a palace to Rose. It was surrounded by a positive forest of gravestones, including several black marble ones. Unconsciously she glanced at Mr Fountain, to find him eyeing her with amusement. Blushing, she fixed her gaze on the graves instead. As they got further up the churchyard path, the stones got larger and more ornate, with gold inlaid in the lettering (*Surely not real gold?* Rose wondered. It looked awfully easy to dig out), and carving all over the tops of them. Closest to the church were a cluster of elaborate tombs, like little temples, with leaf-topped pillars and heavily locked doors. The funny thing was that they were covered in carvings of people in old-fashioned clothes – not quite like Bible story ones, but almost. Yet the faces didn't look as beautiful as the clothes. They were portraits of real people, of the families the tombs belonged to. Rose could see that the sculptor had tried to make them look grand and dignified, but that woman there in the draped tunic, she looked as though she should have a smart hat on, with fruit on it, and you could see from her frown that she'd been thinking about getting rid of the laundrymaid.

Rose jumped as a hand shot out and hauled her away. 'Come on!' Susan snapped. 'I'm supposed to be making sure you behave, you little brat.'

The church was nothing like the one they'd been to at the orphanage. That had had plain white-washed walls, scratched wooden pews, and only one stained-glass window, depicting a rather heavily coloured portrait of St John with an eagle. It always looked as though the eagle was considering pecking off his ear.

Here *every* window was coloured, filled with saints, all standing in niches, each either side of a larger panel. The sun shone through the rich, dark colours, making Rose's eyes water. The stone floor of the church was filled with puddles of jewelled light.

'This is my favourite.' Sarah nudged her as the servants filed up a narrow stair into a gallery that ran around the sides and back of the church. 'Moses in the bulrushes. Look!'

Rose looked at the little window obediently. It *was* pretty. The bulrushes waved in the breeze off the river, but Rose didn't think it was that special. Although, the way the bulrushes were painted was very clever. They almost looked as though they were moving...

They *were* moving. And the water was rippling. And baby Moses was waving a fist out of the blanket across his basket. Rose gasped. It was like her moving pictures! So *this* was what Sarah had meant by watching the glass.

'Is it magic?' she whispered to Sarah, who leaned close, and whispered back in her ear, keeping an eye on Miss Bridges.

'Of course. Lots of magicians' families come to this church. They give the magic for them. Mr Fountain did Moses parting the Red Sea, over by the pulpit.' Sarah jerked her head over, and Rose saw the window she meant. It was the biggest one in the church. The water drew back in a foaming wall to let the trembling Israelites – one of whom looked remarkably like Isabella – scurry through. Then it crashed back down on the Egyptian soldiers, there was an odd shimmer, and the scene went back to the way it had been before. Rose stared at it thoughtfully. It wasn't quite like her pictures then. This was just a tiny snatch of a story that repeated itself again and again. But it did seem that what she could do was magic of a kind.

The service was very long. The vicar of St John's had tailored his services to his flock, which was the children of St Bridget and St Bartholomew, and very few others. This church, by contrast, was packed with society folk, magicians, and intellectuals, who liked a long, grand service, full of processions and choirs and swirling censers. The smell of the incense made Rose sleepy, and the flickering windows made it hard to concentrate. At the orphanage they had been examined on the sermon, but discreet questioning of Sarah and Bill had shown that was not the case in the Fountain house.

Rose stayed sitting up straight, but she relaxed inside, and let herself think about the last week. Miss Bridges' dislike of idleness and the busy hubbub of the kitchens had made it impossible to just sit and think. She was far too tired to stay awake at night – she could hardly drag herself up the stairs as it was. She heard only fragments of the long prayers, in the vicar's slow, sonorous voice.

'We pray for His Majesty, King Albert. We pray for the Royal Family, our dear Princesses…

'We pray for the health of our dear sister, Jane Wetherly…

'We pray for the safety of Emmeline Chambers, disappeared from her home, and Lucinda Mayne, likewise…'

Idly, Rose wondered if Emmeline and Lucinda had run off to join the circus, like Bill's friend Jack… Oh, what was she going to do about this stupid magic? The pictures had been bad enough, but at least they hadn't been discovered. The treacle could have been a disaster.

What if the angry gentleman had managed to grab her and haul her back to the house, demanding an explanation? She would have been sent straight back to the orphanage.

She simply had to get rid of it. Take it out of herself somehow. Surely she could do that, if she didn't want it any more? She could hide it in a box under her bed, perhaps.

Rose sighed. She had a horrible feeling it wouldn't be that easy. The pictures had felt like part of her, and the episode of the treacle – well, it had just *happened*. She had done it without even meaning to. How could she steal the magic out of herself when she didn't know where it was, or what? *Please let that Prendergast book tell me how!* Rose prayed fiercely.

The service ended at last, and the family stayed to gossip with the fashionable crowd. Miss Bridges exchanged stately compliments with Mrs Lark from across the square, and the maids pointed out the most awful bonnets and giggled over them.

'Where has Mrs Jones gone?' Rose asked Sarah. 'Did she go home? Does she have to make the lunch?' She was surprised that Sarah hadn't been sent to do it.

'No, no, it's all cold food on a Sunday. We aren't supposed to work, you know.' Sarah sniffed dismissively. 'Not work! Hah! But at least the jobs are

99

mostly done.' She looked across the churchyard. 'No, I thought so. She's over there, Rose, look.'

Miss Bridges saw them, and frowned. 'Rose, could you go and fetch Mrs Jones? We should leave now. My apologies to her, please.'

Rose nodded, and set off at a run. Realising after a few steps that she was probably committing sacrilege by running in a churchyard, she slowed to a brisk walk, turning the strange little scene over in her mind. What was Mrs Jones doing? Why should Miss Bridges apologise?

But as soon as she drew level with Mrs Jones, she understood. The cook was standing by a tiny headstone, in the far corner of the churchyard. This was no society memorial, just a cheap little grey stone tablet.

Maria Rose Jones

Departed this life aged two months

It was a very brief message. But then Rose had a feeling that stonemasons might have to be paid by the letter.

'Oh, Rose, did they send you to bring me? I'm sorry, dear.'

'Mrs Jones…is that…is that your baby?' Rose asked in a whisper.

Mrs Jones set off down the path, dabbing at her eyes.

'Yes, Rose. She would have been your age now, you know. It was the cholera took her, and her father too, a week later. I couldn't afford another stone – his name's on the back of the baby's. I went back into service after that, I couldn't see anything else to do. Luckily my old place took me back.'

'Oh.' Rose couldn't think of anything else to say, though it didn't feel like she'd said enough.

'It reminds me, Rose,' Mrs Jones muttered, starting to search in her reticule. 'Where's the blasted thing got to – beg pardon, Lord – ah!' She pulled out an odd little muslin bag that smelled strongly of rosemary, and other, unfamiliar, herbs. 'You'd best have this, Rose. I don't really approve of this sort of thing – magic ought to stay in its place, that's what I say, but needs must. It was given me by – well, by someone who knows about these things. Look after it careful, mind.'

'What is it?' Rose asked, taking the little bag gingerly. It had a cord on it, for wearing round her neck, she guessed.

'Why, it's an amulet, dear. I forget you know nothing about this silly magic lark. Don't you worry, Rose, you're better off that way. It's for protection. Now just you tuck it away, I can see Miss Bridges tapping her foot from here. But I'd never forgive myself if you got snatched, when you're out shopping. Two more little girls this morning, did you hear? I don't know what the world's coming to. And all these magicians listening to the vicar. Are they doing anything? No, they are not, Rose, I can tell you that much.'

Rose obediently tucked the amulet in the pocket of her cloak, but she didn't think it would do anything. She knew, by now, what magic things felt like. There were certain things in the house that shimmered as her eyes fell on them, or she could hear them humming. She was practically certain that this was a bag of rather smelly herbs, and nothing more.

'What's happening to those girls, Mrs Jones?' she asked anxiously.

'Oh, my dear, stolen by slavers, I shouldn't wonder. Bloodthirsty pirates, stealing up the river in the dead of night.' Mrs Jones shuddered dramatically, and Rose got the feeling she was quite enjoying herself.

SEVEN

A bell jangled frantically in the corner of the kitchen, and everyone looked up, irritably. It was the middle of Monday morning, washing day, and the copper wouldn't light properly. Tempers were fraying quite quickly, and no one wanted to have to deal with the family right now.

Susan craned her neck to look at the bells. 'It's the workroom. Mr Fountain's up there giving Mr Freddie his lessons.'

'Who knows what they've done now! Rose, you go and see what they want,' Miss Bridges snapped. 'Bill, get out from under there, you'll set your ears on fire.'

Rose dashed up the stairs as fast as she could. The bell was still ringing, and she could feel the urgency

103

and irritation behind it, as though it were screaming at her. She knocked on the workroom door and went in, curtseying to Mr Fountain.

He was standing in the middle of the floor, surrounded by smashed glass and looking furious. 'Ah, good. Rose. Sweep this up, would you? As for you, idiot boy, be grateful I don't make you do it yourself. You must *listen…*'

Rose backed quietly out of the room, and ran downstairs again to fetch brushes.

'Broken glass,' she reported to Miss Bridges. 'Ever such a lot of it, Miss, it might take me a while.'

Miss Bridges just waved her away with a long-suffering look. 'I cannot believe there is a mouse's nest in the copper! Do we not have traps? Where is that dratted cat when we want him?'

Rose grinned to herself. At the moment, even sweeping up broken glass looked better than being below stairs.

When she got back to the workroom, she crept in through the open door. Mr Fountain had gone back to teaching Freddie, and they were both standing by the big wooden table, fiddling with some complicated arrangement of glass tubes.

Rose looked at them worriedly. They were right in the middle of all that broken glass. Even with the best boots on, which she was sure theirs were, their feet could still be cut to ribbons. She was about to mention it, very humbly, when she noticed that actually, their feet weren't touching the ground at all. They were floating, their boot-soles quite an inch above the glass. Neither of them seemed to be bothered about it. They weren't even looking at their feet. Mr Fountain was explaining something to Freddie, and Freddie was staring at the glass tubes, with his nose practically next to them.

'Can you see it? There, look!' Mr Fountain pointed at something. 'Did you see?'

Freddie shook his head. 'No, Sir, I'm sorry. It's too quick.'

Mr Fountain huffed in exasperation. 'Again…'

Rose started to sweep up the glass, very carefully. She was aware that this glass was the remnant of some strange magical experiment, and she wasn't sure it was safe to touch. What might it turn her into? One of the things that was too fast for Freddie to see?

As she swept around them, Mr Fountain and Freddie helpfully rose a couple more inches off the floor, and Rose murmured her thanks. At last she tipped the last of the glass into the newspaper she'd brought, and parcelled it up. She straightened her back, sighing a little. It ached from standing bent over her brush.

'You see it now, Freddie?' Mr Fountain asked, as they

lightly touched down to the ground, without even thinking about it, as far as Rose could see.

'I…think so…' Freddie said slowly, and Rose gasped, 'Oh!' She had just seen what they were looking at. Inside the glass tubes was a soft, silvery mist, pulsing and wavering, now here, now there. It was beautiful. And it had heard her, she was sure. It oiled smoothly round the tubing until it was at the closest point to Rose, and looked at her. It didn't have eyes, but she knew it was looking. It was obvious.

Rose suddenly realised that it wasn't only the mist looking at her. Mr Fountain and Freddie were staring at her, too, Mr Fountain with an expression of great interest, and Freddie with his pale eyebrows drawn together in a furious scowl.

Of course, if he could hardly see the mist, and now the servant girl was standing looking at it like it was jumping up and down and waving banners at her, he *would* be annoyed. Rose backed away apologetically, and scurried out of the room, but she could feel Mr Fountain's interested gaze stuck to her back all the way down the stairs.

Rose kept remembering that silvery mist while she was helping Mrs Trump mangle the washing. Her arms ached from turning the handle, but she almost didn't notice. She wondered what it was, the misty stuff. It was so pretty. She sighed lightly. It might be nice, to do things like that with magic. She almost wished...

Then she looked up, and saw Bill standing there with another basket of wet washing. He was watching her, with an odd expression, rather suspicious. It made him look rattier than ever. But it reminded Rose that she did *not* want to do magic. Ever. She wanted to be a real person.

Rose was kept hard at work all morning helping with the washing, but Mrs Trump departed after lunch, leaving the servants' quarters swathed in damp and steaming garments. She would be back the next day for the ironing. The atmosphere below stairs seemed to lighten, even though everyone was pink with the heat of the copper.

In the middle of the afternoon, Miss Bridges snipped off the last thread from Rose's new pink-striped cotton dress with her little stork-shaped scissors, and sighed. 'There!' She looked up at the clock in the corner of the servants' hall. 'You may have half an hour to yourself, Rose, before you need to take tea to Miss Isabella and Miss Anstruther in the schoolroom.' She smiled. 'Everyone else in the house will be resting, so you should too.'

Rose blinked, a tiny glimmer of a plan nagging in her mind. 'The master and – and the others all have a rest now, then?' she asked, trying hard not to sound too interested. She had been kept so busy, she hardly knew what she was doing, let alone anyone else.

'Yes, although of course Mr Fountain is at Court this afternoon. He has rooms there too, you see.'

Rose nodded. Here was her chance. If she was quick, she could nip up to the workroom and consult that book without anyone noticing. She'd kept trying to get a look at it, but Mr Freddie seemed to have a genius for lurking where she didn't want him to be, and she'd had to pretend she'd been sent to sweep the floor an unconvincing number of times.

She whisked up the stairs, trying to tread lightly, and crept up to the door. It was humming. Not a pleasant sort of noise, such as she might make while polishing something, but an odd, almost malevolent buzz. Like a swarm of evil bees. *Bad bees.* Rose suppressed a nervous giggle. She was being silly, but whatever was happening in the workroom was not good. And she didn't think it was anything as simple as bees, either. Something horrible was going on in there. Rose put her hand to her mouth and nibbled the side of her thumb worriedly. Should she just go? What if this was one of those vital-to-the-nation things that Miss Bridges had mentioned, and she would break it somehow if she opened the door? She really didn't *want* to open the door, anyway... Unfortunately, this was just the thing that told her she probably should. She wasn't being nosy, she could sense that this wasn't right, and she had to do something about it.

Silently cursing this strange magical house, Rose put her hand on the doorknob. It was icy, and yet it seemed to burn her fingers as she twisted it. Rose pushed the door open quickly, before her feet could give up and run away.

Freddie was standing in the middle of the room. He was clutching Gustavus the cat in his arms, and both of them were stone-still. Their eyes were round with fear, which is not that hard for a cat, but very difficult for a boy.

Wreathing round them was a strange, black shadow – or was it a smoke, or a mist? Rose couldn't tell, and it seemed to change even as she looked at it. It had eyes, she noticed, with a sudden chill. And now they were looking at her. Rose realised in horror that it was the pretty mist she'd seen that morning. Only it wasn't pretty, it was horrible, and alien. The eerie vapour poured itself across the room to rush at Rose, and instinctively she put up her hands to protect her face, and closed her eyes.

There was a strange, irritated note to the buzzing

now, grumpy almost, and Rose ventured to open one eye slowly. The smoke-creature was six inches away from her, hissing in frustration, and clearly unable to get any closer. Rose stared at it, confused. Then she caught a twitch of movement in the corner of her eye, and flicked a glance at Freddie. He was free, or at least his eyes were. He and Gustavus were peering hopefully, anxiously, at Rose and the mist-monster, and Gustavus was starting to be able to twitch his tail.

Why didn't the creature freeze her too, or do whatever it was it had done to the others? Had it perhaps used up all its power? Rose looked at it uncertainly, and back at Freddie. What should she *do*? The strange being saw her glance, and whirled round in a misty, angry coil. It shot back to Freddie and the cat, or it would have done, if Rose hadn't grabbed it. She did it without thinking. If she'd thought, she would have known you couldn't grab mist. But she had. It was buzzing, almost shrieking round her hand, biting and scratching, though without teeth or claws that she could see. It hurt.

Rose hit it. She had fought other girls a few times at the orphanage – not many, for she was one of the quiet ones – and she was well able to take care of herself. No smoke was going to bite her and get away with it. Besides, she could feel its nastiness trying to seep into her skin with the bites. She wasn't having that. She only had half an hour, and then she had to be serving tea. 'Stop it!' she snapped, and cuffed the creature round where she guessed its ear should be. And it did. In fact, it vanished, leaving Rose feeling rather disappointed.

She gazed confusedly at the space where it had been, then looked up at Freddie and Gustavus.

They were staring at her, open-mouthed, as though she had just single-handedly dispatched a phantom. Which, Rose supposed, she had.

EIGHT

'What did you do?' Freddie demanded. He sounded furious, and he looked as though he'd rather like to grab Rose, and shake the truth out of her. But he still couldn't move properly. Whatever the mist-creature had done to him and Gustavus was taking time to wear off.

As soon as the creature had disappeared, Rose had run towards them, wanting to help, but now she took a doubtful step back. 'I – I don't know,' she admitted. 'What was it, anyway? Where'd it come from?'

'None of your business!' Freddie shouted. His face was white, but with angry red spots on his cheeks, and his dark eyes were glittering angrily – as though he was trying not to cry from embarrassment, and rage.

Rose had to try hard not to smile. He couldn't stand

her seeing him like this, couldn't bear it that she, an ignorant little servant-girl, had actually rescued him. She almost felt sorry for him, but not quite.

'Frederick, she just saved us,' the cat said reprovingly. He was now sitting on the big table again, as he had been that morning, and frantically washing. He only took his paw away from his mouth for a few seconds, then he was back to licking and swiping. Rose could understand why. She felt as though she was covered in a strange sticky, prickly film herself, and she didn't have fur.

'No, she didn't!' Freddie had himself more under control by now, and he was no longer shouting. He spoke quietly, but his voice was frozen with fury. It made Rose shiver.

'Of course she did!' Gustavus actually stopped washing for long enough to glare at him this time.

'All she did was walk in and distract it,' Freddie insisted. 'We saved ourselves. And don't talk in front of her, she's a servant!'

'A servant who can hear me,' the cat pointed out. 'All the rest of them would think they heard a cat mewing. Which just goes to show, doesn't it?' He rubbed his paw over his ear roughly, muttering disgustedly to himself.

Freddie looked around the room desperately, while he tried to think what to say. 'So she can understand cat,' he said at last. 'That doesn't mean anything…'

Rose wished they would stop talking as though she wasn't there, but she didn't dare say anything. Freddie was Mr Fountain's apprentice, and Gustavus was his spoilt pet. If they complained of her, she might be sent back to the orphanage.

'She just interrupted that creature when it was weak from binding us, that's all,' Freddie said more confidently. 'It was nothing to do with her, really.'

Rose watched Gustavus give Freddie a considering look, then the cat turned his parti-coloured eyes on her. 'Where did you learn to hear cats talk, girl?'

Rose shook her head. 'I don't know. I never knew they could. The cat at the orphanage never said anything, not that I heard. You just talked to me about the cream that first morning I saw you. Last week.'

The cat sniffed. 'Who knows. You wouldn't expect a servant child to have magic—'

'Magic!' Freddie interrupted scornfully. 'Of course she doesn't have magic. Little guttersnipe. Like I said, it was luck. Coincidence. And maybe she stole something from in here that made her understand you. Yes, I bet that's it! What did you take, girl?' He rounded on her, working himself into a rage to beat down his fear.

Rose stood her ground. 'I never stole anything, and you know it!' She was past the point of not wanting to get on his bad side by now. It was too late, and she hated him too much to hold back, anyway. 'And if you say I did,' – Rose leaned forwards and jabbed a finger in his chest – 'I'll tell your master what I just saw, because I'll bet my year's wages you weren't supposed to be messing with that mist thing.'

Freddie gaped at her. He clearly had no experience of servants talking back. They usually just moaned about him once he'd gone. 'You wouldn't dare,' he hissed, but with an edge of doubt.

Rose raised an eyebrow at him, and the cat sniggered. 'She's got you there, Freddie.'

'You helped,' Freddie retorted. 'And Fountain will know that; he knows I couldn't do that spell on my own. I could hardly even see the thing this morning.'

'You *brought* it here?' Rose asked disgustedly. 'What on earth were you thinking?'

'We were experimenting,' Freddie told her in a lordly way. 'Testing our power, as is natural for those who hold the secrets of the mages. Which you would know if you had any magic at all,' he added, suddenly sounding much less grown up. 'I don't know how you can talk to Gustavus, but apart from that you're the least magical person I've ever met.'

'Really? Are you sure?' Rose asked hopefully. She wanted to believe him so much. She wanted to be safe downstairs in the warm kitchen, away from buzzing things, with everyone else who thought those magicians were more trouble than they were worth. She did not want to be one of the troublemakers.

'It was coincidence, that's all. Like I said,' Freddie told her firmly. A little bit of Rose couldn't help wondering if he was trying to convince himself as much as he was trying to persuade her. But he was a magician's apprentice. He could summon monsters, even if he did have to be rescued from them afterwards. His dark eyes were wide and sincere now, and Rose felt herself wrapped in their velvety blackness. He looked so certain. He must know. He *did* know.

Rose dropped a little curtsey. 'Thank you, Sir,' she murmured. 'I'm so sorry to have interrupted your…studies.' She couldn't quite hold back a laugh on the last word, but she was staring at her boots, like a model servant.

Freddie glared at her, his fingers clenched into fists, but he said nothing.

'Thank you, girl!' the cat called after her as she opened the door. 'I'll be down for some salmon later, if you please!'

Rose clicked the door shut, and leaned against it for a second. That hadn't been what she planned to happen, not at all. But at least she knew it wasn't magic that was making all these strange things keep happening to her.

Magic was messy and difficult and not her place to know. She was having nothing to do with it.

So how do *you make pictures on bathtubs?* a little voice demanded in her head. *And pour treacle on men on big horses? And why can't Bill and the others hear the cat?* But Rose was very carefully not listening. It was too nice, knowing that she was normal after all. She didn't want anything to spoil it.

By the time she'd helped Bill fetch all the shoes for cleaning, and taken Miss Anstruther her bedtime cocoa (Mrs Jones had laced it with brandy), Rose was exhausted. Even her pretty china candlestick felt too heavy to carry up the shadowy stairs. She was too weary to care if the steps stretched and weaved beneath her. It was only that she was tired, and the candle flame was flickering. She was imagining it, like Bill had said. All she wanted to do now was get to her little room and sleep.

She jerked awake sometime in the blackest part of the night, quite certain that someone was in the room with her. She could hear breathing. At once she was convinced that it was the mist-creature back again, she could feel it, it was swirling over her face, coiling round her throat, about to rush into her mouth and nose and suffocate her—

'She's going to scream,' an interested voice remarked from next to her left ear.

'Don't!' This voice was panicked, and familiar. Freddie.

'What are you doing in my room?' Rose hissed angrily. She was quite shocked. The matrons at St Bridget's would have had fits about this, and she couldn't imagine Miss Bridges being very happy either.

'It's all right, I brought Gustavus as a chaperon,' Freddie explained reassuringly. There was a rustling noise, which turned out to be Freddie getting a candle stub from his dressing gown pocket, and blowing on it. It flared at once, lighting up Freddie's pale, ghostly face, and the white cat perched on the edge of Rose's pillow.

'A chaperon! He's a cat! And nobody else can hear him!' Rose snarled. Somehow Freddie's easy, thoughtless display of magic made her hate him even more. 'Get out! And how did you get in, anyway?' she added, imagining them flying in through the window on a magic carpet. But the window was shut.

'We walked up the stairs and opened the door,' Gustavus said wearily.

'Actually, I carried you, because you were moaning so much. And he's awfully heavy. Can I sit down?' Freddie made to sit on the end of her bed.

'NO!' Rose pulled the bedclothes up to her chin in horror.

'But we need to talk to you, and I can't stand up for much longer, there isn't room. I'm practically sitting in your washstand at the moment. Your bedroom is *tiny*.'

'You get out of it, and it'll be just right!' Rose snapped.

'Oh, let him sit, girl. He'll just whinge, otherwise.' Gustavus yawned, showing rows of white teeth like needles. 'He's come to apologise, you know,' he added persuasively.

'Have you?' Rose asked, forgetting to be cross. She was too surprised.

'Only because Gus said he'd tell if I didn't,' Freddie muttered, tucking himself onto the end of the bed.

Rose nodded. She would have been suspicious of any other answer. 'What're you apologising for? Calling me a thief? Or for making me sweep that floor over, when it was spotless first time round?'

There was an uncomfortable silence.

'Tell her,' the cat insisted.

'All right!' Freddie glared at Rose and Gustavus. 'I lied to you. You did save us. There, happy now?' he asked the cat.

'No.' Rose and the cat said it together, and the cat added, 'You should grovel. Make him grovel, girl, you saved his skin.'

Rose shook her head. 'No, I just interrupted that – thing. That's all. You said so.'

'And I was lying, like I said.' Freddie looked up at her, the candlelight making great shadows round his eyes. He clearly hated to admit it. 'You did save us by magic. I don't know how,' he added grudgingly.

'I didn't!' Rose protested. 'How could I? I don't know anything about magic. And you were so sure. You said I was the least magical person you'd ever met.'

'Well, you are.' Freddie shrugged. 'But you still did it. We were trapped, and you rescued us.'

'It must have been a coincidence, like you said,' Rose said hopefully. 'I didn't actually do anything. I can't.'

Freddie sighed irritably. 'Look, I know I lied, and I suppose I did do a little bit of a persuading spell on you back in the workroom, but now I promise I'm telling the truth. It *was* you, and you used proper magic. Lots of it. More than I've ever managed to find. Oh, come on, how can you not *know*?'

Rose just stared at him silently. She couldn't think of anything to say, apart from no, and he didn't seem to be hearing that.

Freddie huffed a long, grumpy breath. 'Why are you so stubborn? I'll prove it, look.' He kneeled up on the bed, and reached over to the little shelf where Rose's candle sat in its china holder. Then he hurled it against the far wall of her room.

Rose gasped, and tried desperately to catch it, but she had no chance. She was all tangled up in the bedclothes, and she was still half asleep, and there was no time anyway.

She waited miserably for the smash, and Susan's angry scream from next door. But it didn't come, and there were no pretty flowered fragments on the floor.

She was holding the candlestick.

Rose looked up at Freddie, and he smiled triumphantly.

'See?'

NINE

Rose gaped at the candlestick. She was very glad it wasn't broken – she would have hated to explain to Miss Bridges that she'd smashed it, in only her second week in the house, and breakages had to come out of her wages. But it *should* have smashed. There was no way she'd caught it. So what was it doing in her hand?

Suddenly she smiled at Freddie. 'That was a spell, wasn't it?' she asked, in a relieved voice. 'You went and mucked about with my mind again. You made me think you'd thrown it, but actually you just handed it to me.'

'No! Look, why would I want to make you think you can do magic when you can't? I just want you back in the kitchens where you belong,' he muttered resentfully.

He sounded very honest. Much more honest than he had earlier on, Rose had to admit. Now she thought about it, it was obvious that he had put some sort of deceiving spell on her before. And it had worked beautifully, because she had wanted to believe him so very much.

Freddie rolled his eyes impatiently, and Gustavus sniggered. 'He isn't that good at sleight of hand, my dear. Elementary conjuring – it still haunts me what came out of that hat...' He looked at Rose eagerly, and seemed to be hoping she would ask him what he meant, but she was hardly listening. She kept running her fingers over the little painted flowers on the candlestick, as though they might tell her what was happening. Then she shuddered. Maybe they would. If cats could talk, who was to say candles couldn't?

At last she looked up at Freddie and the cat. 'Don't worry,' she said calmly. 'That's where I'll be, just the same as usual.'

'Where? What are you talking about?' Freddie said, glaring at her. He still seemed to be taking her magic as a personal insult.

'In the kitchens, where I belong. I don't want to have magic in me,' Rose insisted. 'I don't like it. Maybe if I just ignore it, it'll go away.'

'It's not some little creature that's taken up residence

inside you for the moment, girl!' Gustavus told her testily. 'It *is* you! You've got it. It doesn't go.'

'It might,' Rose said stubbornly.

Freddie was staring at her as though she was a dangerous lunatic. 'But – don't you want it?' he asked, his voice dazed. 'I thought you just didn't understand. Don't you know how *lucky* you are?'

'Yes,' Rose hissed. 'Yes, I do know! I've got a job! A week ago I went from being an orphan with no proper name to being somebody who earns money. *That's* lucky! That's what I wanted! Not spells, and misty-monsters leaping at me!'

'It was an elemental spirit, actually,' Freddie said under his breath, as though he couldn't help putting her right.

'Whatever!' Rose snapped. 'I still don't want anything to do with it.'

Freddie gave Gustavus a hopeful look. 'I don't suppose she could give it to me, could she? Old Fountain would have a heart attack.'

Gustavus glared at him. 'Don't be any more stupid than you have to, boy,' he growled. 'The power is hers, and that's the way it stays – whether you both like it or not. I'd still like to know where you got it from, though,' he added, in a much less grumpy voice. 'Is there any magic in your family?'

Rose shrugged. 'How should I know? I'm an orphan, remember?'

'You really don't know anything about your parents?' Freddie sounded disbelieving.

'Do you think I'm making this up?' Rose asked wearily. 'I don't *like* being an orphan! All I know is they dumped me in the churchyard. In a fishbasket,' she added, very quietly, because she knew Freddie would laugh.

He did, but Rose and Gustavus gave him such a dirty look that he stopped quite quickly.

'Fish is very good,' the cat told her consolingly. 'Quite my favourite food.'

It didn't help, but Rose appreciated that he was trying to be kind, and smiled at him.

Gustavus swayed slightly, and blinked, his whiskers trembling. 'Charm,' he muttered to Freddie. 'You see? It gets you a long way. Look after that smile, child. Tooth-cleaning powder… Where was I?'

'Being bewitched by Little Miss Perfect's smile,' Freddie snapped. 'Don't ever teach her to flutter her eyelashes. And don't worry,' he warned Rose, 'it definitely won't work on me. Gus is a soppy old fool. So what are we going to do?'

'Do?' Rose looked at him with dislike. 'I'd like to go back to sleep, please. Some of us have to be up at six, to light *your* bedroom fire. Which you could very well do by yourself. You wouldn't even have to get out of bed.'

Freddie ignored her. 'When are we going to tell old Fountain?' he murmured. 'I suppose I'd better come too, or he'll never believe you. And you, Gus.'

'No!' Rose squeaked in horror. 'I'm not telling anyone, and neither are you!'

'But you need to tell him. He'll have to train you, I should think, since you were discovered in his house. That's how it works with new magic, isn't it, Gus?'

'Mmmm. One of the basic responsibilities of a magician.' The cat nodded, his whiskers waving regally. 'Training. She'll probably have to be another apprentice.'

'Oh, excellent! She can do all the measuring!' Freddie looked distinctly more cheerful at the thought of having someone to boss around.

'Did he discover you, then?' Rose asked curiously.

Freddie shook his head. 'No. Fountain was at the university with my father. He took me as a favour. Most magicians have at least one apprentice, and they agreed it when I was born, I think. Probably my father will train Isabella, if she's any good. It's harder to tell with girls. Usually. Isabella has an unnatural talent for torturing governesses, but that may be all she's good at.'

Rose nodded. 'Well, I don't want to be trained, so it

doesn't matter. You're not telling him.'

Freddie shrugged. 'You can tell him if you like, but I don't think he'll believe you. Look, I'm sorry to say this, but you're a servant. Servants don't *do* magic. No one's going to believe that you can. Fountain will think it's some sort of trick. He'll probably sack you on the spot.'

'No, he won't, because I'm not telling him either,' Rose explained patiently. 'Like I said, I'm not telling anyone, and neither are you.'

Freddie narrowed his eyes. 'You mean, you're just going to carry on being – a skivvy? When you could be a magician? Are you insane? Do you know how much a certified magician *earns*?'

'No,' Rose admitted. 'But I know how to scrub floors, and I don't know anything about magic. And I don't want to!' she added stubbornly. 'It's scary and difficult, and like you said, I'm a servant and I'm not supposed to do it. So I won't.' She eyed Freddie thoughtfully. 'Unless you tell someone, in which case I will do something, and I don't know what and it'll probably go very wrong and no one will be able to fix it, so just don't. All right?'

Freddie held his hands up. 'Fine! I won't mention it. You can just let it all go to waste, and we won't say a thing.' He slid off the bed and stood up, scooping

Gustavus into his arms. 'Come on, you.' He stomped the two steps to the door, then he paused and looked back. 'Just this once, I'll do the fire tomorrow,' he allowed her grudgingly.

Rose smiled as he closed the door. *My magic must be powerful*, she mused sleepily. *He wouldn't do that unless he really was impressed.*

128

TEN

Rose found herself looking forward to cleaning the workroom the next day. She wanted to look at the books, and all those strange pieces of equipment. However much she'd told Freddie she didn't care about the magic, it was impossible to forget. She'd suspected before, but now she *knew* and it coloured everything. She'd even wondered if she could turn Susan into a newt when she'd thrown a boot at her to wake her that morning. It was probably a good thing Rose didn't know how to use the magic. It would be just too tempting.

But when she got into the kitchen after doing all the fires, Rose found that the morning routine had suddenly changed. She was late for the servants'

breakfast anyway, as she'd had to go back to Miss Isabella's room to take her more biscuits. Isabella had come screaming out of her bedroom just as Rose was thinking she'd finished, because the ones in her tin were 'hateful currant ones that are full of squashed flies and I shan't eat them so there!' Rose had run back up with shortbread instead, only to find Isabella sitting smugly cross-legged in bed, munching a plain biscuit, and watching a swarm of currant-sized black flies buzzing sadly round her bedposts.

'You'd better get rid of them,' she told Rose sweetly, and it took Rose ten minutes to shoo them all out of the window with a feather duster. She wasn't sure how long they would last outside, since they were really just currants with wings, but she didn't have time to worry about them. She slammed down the window, and gave Miss Isabella a *look*.

'Will there be anything else, Miss?' she asked very politely through her teeth.

Isabella stared back haughtily, but perhaps she decided she had done enough. 'No-o. Not this minute. I shall ring, if I need you.'

Rose trudged into the kitchen, feeling hollow inside, and hoping that Bill hadn't eaten all the porridge. But no one was eating. Everyone was staring at a strange glassy bubble that was floating in the middle of the table. It held a weirdly curved image of Mr Fountain, and a scratchy little voice was coming from it, repeating the same message over and over again.

Pickled herrings for breakfast, please. And don't burn the toast. Pickled herrings for breakfast, please. And don't burn the toast.

Mrs Jones was glaring at it with her hands on her hips. 'When do I ever send him up burnt toast? What's come over the man? I don't have any pickled herrings. Oh, will someone please get rid of that thing!' she squawked at last.

'How?' Bill asked. He looked at Rose, but she avoided his eye. Susan was poking at the bubble gingerly with a fork, but it just floated away, still demanding pickled herrings.

Then Gustavus trotted into the kitchen, whiskers twitching and clearly hoping for cream. He eyed the bubble with his head on one side, then leaped lightly onto the table. He batted at the bubble as though it were a butterfly he was chasing, patting it from paw to paw in the most delicate fashion. Then he lunged, and snatched it in his teeth. It squeaked feebly – *herrings!* – and deflated, trailing from one corner of his mouth like a scrap of fish skin before it disappeared down his gullet. Gustavus licked his chops, and winked at Rose.

Mrs Bridges sat down heavily, and extended a shaking

131

hand to pat his ears. 'You good cat,' she murmured. Gus even purred for her. Clearly he was very anxious for cream. Rose filled the saucer to the brim, and Gus sat on her lap to drink it.

'Rose, you'll have to go out for the herrings, dear,' Mrs Jones said, after a few gulps of tea. 'Oh, dearie me, it's really turned my stomach, that thing. I feel quite odd.'

Rose looked around the kitchen. Sarah was ashen, and Bill looked grim. Susan, who was so fierce, had the back of her hand to her mouth as though she felt sick. Rose felt confused. It wasn't really that scary, was it? It was only a talking picture. *Like my pictures*, she thought. She couldn't understand how they could all live in Mr Fountain's house, but still be so afraid of his magic. Only Miss Bridges seemed unshaken, and even she was clearly irritated.

'Sarah, cut Rose some bread and butter. Hurry back, Rose, and we'll keep you some breakfast. Really, why he couldn't have mentioned it yesterday. It's just a mercy he breakfasts late.'

Rose came back from the fishmonger's pink-cheeked. The boy behind the counter had been particularly rude, asking if she'd like a free lobster with her herrings now, to save her the trouble of coming back to complain. Oddly, all the lobsters seemed to have got very lively after that, and several of them had lost the bindings on their claws. Rose watched them through the window, determinedly climbing down the counter, and under the petticoats of a bad-tempered old lady buying a kipper. When she'd come into the shop, she'd complained about having to wait, and made loud comments about Rose being no better than she should be, flirting with shop boys like a shameless hussy. Seeing the lobsters disappear under her skirt cheered Rose up so much she almost forgot she was starving, and she raced all the way home with the herrings, wanting to tell Bill the joke.

She was crossing the square at a run when she realised that all the lobsters couldn't have come untied at once. *She* had untied them, without knowing it. She slowed to a walk, turning it over in her mind anxiously. Another thing she'd done without realising. The magic just kept popping out and *doing* things, and she had no idea how to stop it. Maybe she did need to learn about it, just to stop herself from doing something awful. She wasn't a bad-tempered person, but she did get cross sometimes. What might she do, without *really* meaning it?

By the time she'd had breakfast it was late, and Miss Bridges said crossly that the workroom had better go undusted for today. Mr Fountain had sent down a message – by the normal means of Susan this time – that he was expecting a visitor for lunch. This was the first anyone had heard of it, and consequently everyone was in a state of flap.

'A lady,' Mrs Jones muttered. 'Mousses. A trifle, perhaps. Blancmange. Oh, I could have made a lovely blancmange, if only he'd given me more time.'

Rose, who was sure that mooses were things with horns that came somewhere in Geography, wondered worriedly if that bubble had turned Mrs Jones's head. But the lunch that was finally sent up was a masterpiece.

'I just hope this lady appreciates it, that's all,' Mrs Jones said irritably, as she subsided into a chair, fanning herself with one hand.

'Who is she?' Rose asked, as Susan paraded smartly out with a large silver soup tureen. She knew Miss Bridges was hovering upstairs, so no one would tell her off for gossiping.

Mrs Jones shrugged. 'Another magician. He's invited her to talk about work, Miss Bridges said.' She looked anxiously over at the jelly sitting on the side table. 'It hasn't had enough time to set properly. They'd better eat their soup and fish quickly, or it'll run away to nothing.'

Rose looked at it admiringly. The pale-pink jelly wobbled on a silver dish, filled with custard inside and decorated with cream and crystallised violets – the ones she and Bill had bought the other day. 'I still don't understand how you got the custard inside the jelly.' She giggled. 'It's like magic!'

Mrs Jones looked at her sharply. 'It most certainly is not, young lady! I told when you arrived, no magic in my kitchen. It's a clever mould, that's all. Magic indeed…'

'I'm sorry, Mrs Jones,' Rose murmured humbly. 'I was joking, I just meant it looks very clever.'

She went out to the back kitchen to help Sarah and Bill wipe up the mass of pans that had been used for cooking lunch, but she was blinking back tears. Mrs Jones had always been so nice to her. Even though the amulet was useless, she'd meant it kindly. What would happen if Mrs Jones found out about Rose's secret? She seemed to dislike magic so much. It was almost as if she found it disgusting. *Everyone will hate me,* Rose thought, a tear dripping off the end of her nose and onto the copper pan she was drying. She rubbed at the smear crossly. *Bill already doesn't know what to say to me. I have to get rid of it.*

Suddenly a loud scream echoed through the house. Rose clapped her hands over her ears. It was like the bell from the workroom – there was magic behind it, making it heard. Pure fury vibrated the windows, and the glass in the cabinets rang.

'What on earth is that?' Sarah gasped.

'Miss Isabella,' Bill predicted. 'Couldn't be anyone else. Wonder who's said no to her now.'

They all flinched as something crashed upstairs, and the bell from the main hallway started to ring frantically.

Sarah and Bill both looked at Rose expectantly. As the newest and youngest servant, it was definitely her job to go. Still in her work-apron, Rose skidded up the stairs to find Miss Bridges standing over a huddle of lace that was drumming its feet on the black-and-white tiled floor. A large china flowerpot was in splinters all over the place, and the fern that had been in it was shredded against the dining room door.

'Fetch brushes, Rose,' Miss Bridges said wearily. 'Isabella, please get up. Rose needs to sweep up this mess, and you might get cut by the porcelain splinters.'

Miss Anstruther, Isabella's governess, came stumbling down the stairs. 'Oh, Miss Bridges, I'm so sorry, Isabella wanted to see her father, and when I said he was busy she locked me in the toy cupboard. Oh, dear, Isabella, what a state you're in.' She looked around helplessly and twisted her hands over and over.

Rose sniffed, very quietly. She pitied Miss Anstruther, but she was so dreadfully wet. She had a sneaking sympathy for Isabella too, shut up with the hand-wringing all the time.

When she came back up with the dustpan, Miss Bridges and Miss Anstruther were still trying to coax Isabella up.

'Come, Isabella, dear, your papa won't want to see you lying here,' Miss Anstruther pleaded. She looked at Miss Bridges, and whispered, 'What happened?'

Not realising that Rose was listening, Miss Bridges explained. 'I told Isabella she couldn't go into the dining room, as Mr Fountain had asked not to be disturbed. But often she's allowed to go and sit with guests for dessert, so she refused to believe me. She slipped past me and opened the door a crack, and then I'm afraid she saw her father's luncheon guest.'

'Oh – the lady magician.' Miss Anstruther nodded. 'Isabella is inclined to be a little jealous.'

'Quite,' Miss Bridges agreed dryly. 'But we need to move her, now. Before they come out. This is quite enough of a disaster already, without Isabella trying to scratch the woman's eyes out.'

'She wouldn't!' Miss Anstruther protested feebly.

Miss Bridges raised her eyebrows. 'Of course she would. How long have you been here?'

A tinkling laugh was heard from inside the dining room, echoed by a man's deeper voice, and Isabella's toes drummed harder on the floor.

Miss Bridges sighed. 'You take her head, I'll have the

feet.' She eyed Isabella's kicking satin slippers ruefully, but Rose thought she probably had the better deal. Isabella looked like she would most definitely bite. She eeled back into the stairway, not wanting to be asked to help.

Miss Bridges was nursing a scratched wrist when she came back down the stairs just as Rose was finishing the floor. 'Good,' she said, looking professionally round for any stray fragments. 'Well done, Rose. Miss Isabella has had a – she's – she has been prostrated by an hysterical collapse.' Miss Bridges coughed. 'Get rid of the remains, and then you may as well go and sweep the workroom, since you had to skip it this morning.'

Rose sighed, and went to parcel up the broken china. This household seemed to get through an awful lot of breakables. She hid herself away in the workroom, not wanting to get involved if Isabella went on the rampage again. Rose was almost sure that her hysterical collapse would only last as long as Miss Bridges and Miss Anstruther were looking.

The kitchen hummed with gossip about Mr Fountain's guest for the rest of the day, and Susan reported eagerly the next morning that he hadn't been to bed – he'd sat up in his study all night, and had worked his way through a whole bottle of the best brandy. Susan also reported that the book on his marble table was *The Compleat Etiquette*, and it had been open to the chapter on marriage proposals. Rose blinked, trying to think back to his room this morning when she'd lit the fire. His bed had had the curtains drawn round it; she hadn't even considered that he might not have been inside.

Isabella had most definitely been in her room. She'd thrown the biscuit barrel at Rose, and had been most upset when Rose caught it. She'd threatened to get her sacked. Clearly, it was an important part of Rose's duties to be concussed by flying china. Rose kept a wary eye out as she set off upstairs again to clean after breakfast. Hopefully she could just clean, and have a little peace and quiet.

Freddie jumped out at her as soon as she got through the workroom door, making her drop her brush. 'Oh good! Have you changed your mind yet?'

'No! You nearly made me break a leg!' Rose started sweeping crossly. She'd wanted time alone in here, to imagine what it would be like to spend her days consulting spellbooks, instead of dusting them.

'Oh, well.' Freddie sighed gloomily. 'Fountain probably wouldn't listen to you anyway, he's too wrapped in that hateful Sparrow woman. He's gone batty about her.' He shook his head. 'I can't understand it, he's only met her about three times. He's got a little portrait of her that he keeps in his waistcoat pocket. I think she gave it to him, and he's spelled it to glow, so he can even see her in the dark!' Freddie snorted with laughter. 'He made me look up the spell after she'd gone.'

'Everyone in the kitchen says he's going to marry her. Susan said she was the most beautiful lady she'd ever seen. Why do you think she's hateful?' Rose asked, leaning on her broom, and looking at him interestedly.

Freddie frowned. Eventually he admitted, 'I don't know. There's just something about her that's wrong. He sent me to fetch some books and things to show her, and she was too grateful. Sort of sweet and honey-ish, but as though the honey's hiding something. Like castor oil. I don't like to look at her,' he added, ducking his head in embarrassment.

'You've got to admit she's beautiful, though,' Gustavus put in.

Rose jumped. He'd been sitting on the windowsill – watching the pigeons, she realised now – and she hadn't seen him.

Freddie shuddered. 'I bet it's a glamour, or most of it is. It must be a very good one though, she never lets it slip, and there's no smell.'

Rose blinked. She had no idea what a glamour was,

and she hadn't intended to ask because she didn't want Freddie to sneer at her again. But a spell with a smell was just too intriguing. She shrugged. 'Go on then. I bet you already know I don't have a clue about any of that. What's a glamour, and why do they smell?'

Freddie had the grace to look apologetic. 'Sorry. After seeing you fight that thing off on Monday, I just forget you don't know all the stuff I do.'

Rose stared at him. He almost sounded as though he were treating her as an equal for a moment – this boy in the velveteen suit, with the exquisitely pressed frilled shirt. For the first time she wondered if this strange gift could really be ignored. Didn't she owe it to someone – she wasn't quite sure who – to do something about it? The orphanage had always been so strict about waste. Miss Lockwood had spread her tea leaves out on a tray every night, so as to dry them out and use them again. Would she approve of Rose letting this opportunity slip by? Rose shook her head slightly, and realised that Freddie had started explaining the glamour thing.

'So other people look at you and see what you want them to see, not what's really there. Of course, it's very difficult, because it has to be kept going all the time. And the thing with glamours is that because they're all to do with twisting people's senses, sometimes you get side effects. People hear a tinkling noise, or there's a funny smell. All the senses, you see?'

Rose nodded. 'Can you do them?' she asked, looking at Freddie's perfectly smooth blond hair, and the dark eyes, with their strange glints of gold. He didn't look all that natural, now she thought about it.

'Of course not!' Freddie laughed. 'I'd have to study for years.'

'I can, though.' Gustavus jumped lightly from the windowsill, and flowed mid-jump into a slim cream-coloured cat, with a black tail and paws. Only the parti-coloured eyes were the same. 'You see? Now I'm a Siamese. And the beauty of it is, *which was I in the first place*? You don't know if I really ought to look like this all the time. That's why glamours are so clever.'

Rose shook her head firmly. 'No. That's not the real one. I've seen the amount you eat.'

Gustavus changed back, looking disgruntled. 'I do *not* eat that much,' he muttered, his ears laid back.

'What you eat would feed at least three orphans,' Rose told him. She smiled. 'I'll tell them about you – oh, not that you can talk, don't worry. It's Wednesday, my first afternoon off. I want to go back and visit.' *And show off*, she admitted to herself.

'What time are you going?' Freddie asked anxiously. 'Miss Sparrow's visiting again this afternoon, I thought you might like to see her. See what a lady magician's like. Not that you want to be like her.'

'I'm not going till later, but I'm still never going to be a lady magician,' said Rose, though her voice was less decided now.

Freddie shrugged. 'Maybe. You should try and catch a glimpse of her though. See if you think there's something odd about her. She reminds me of a spider.'

Rose nodded. She didn't like spiders either; the scuttling way they moved made her heart thump most unpleasantly. But she was very good at chasing them away with a broom.

Rose wasn't supposed to be seen by guests – she was a below-stairs servant, and only allowed to wait on the children. Susan did the answering of doors, and serving of meals. But Freddie slipped into the kitchen just after lunch, looking apologetic, with a story about a broken jar that needed sweeping up. After the episode with the Ming vase, Miss Bridges was so eager to get rid of That Boy that she positively pushed Rose and a dustpan out of the kitchen after him.

'Were you making her do that?' Rose asked. She was starting to see Freddie's magic as more and more useful – if only as a substitute for low cunning.

'No, she just really doesn't like me.' He didn't seem worried. 'Come on, we can lurk on the stairs, and

I've even got a jar to break, look!'

'Do we have to?' Rose protested. 'I'll be the one sweeping it up, won't I?'

'We have to have something, in case they see us,' Freddie said patiently. 'Oh, all right, we'll break it in the dustpan, then you can pretend to have just finished.'

He produced a delicate little silver hammer, and had just smashed the jar into pieces in the dustpan when the doorbell rang. He nearly spilt them all anyway, peering over the banisters.

'It's her,' he hissed, as they watched Susan trotting to the door and straightening her cap as she went. 'I can see her hat through the glass, those enormous ostrich feathers.'

In the event, all Rose saw of Miss Alethea Sparrow was three tall, nodding ostrich plumes, and a smart purple coat drawn in tight to the waist. There was only a glimpse of a pale, pointed face, and dark ringlets. But Rose didn't need to see more to agree with Freddie's description. She *was* like a spider. Rose wanted to draw her skirts in, and hide behind a broom – preferably with someone else holding it. Poor Mr Fountain, as he came exclaiming and fussing out of the drawing room towards her, was nothing more than a besotted fly.

ELEVEN

It was very odd to walk through the streets alone, and to know that she looked like a well-dressed servant girl, and not an object of pity. Rose *was* a well-dressed servant girl. She had newish boots, now, and a bonnet that fitted.

Bill had drawn her a map of the way back to the orphanage, which she was clutching tightly in her gloved hand (her, Rose, wearing gloves!). She walked along the pavement beside the garden in the square. She hadn't had time to stop and look when she'd been running after Miss Bridges, and Bill had hustled her along too quickly to look at it properly when they'd gone shopping. The garden was empty of children today, but an elderly lady sat on a bench, watching a fussy little black dog chase and snap at butterflies. The statues were all of elderly gentlemen, now she had time to look at them, and one had a large stone bird perched on his shoulder. Rose wondered if he was a magician, too – the bird didn't look like an ordinary pet. It had a cruel, curved beak, and even though its eyes were stone it seemed to be looking at her. Rose shuddered and walked on quickly. When she glanced back, she was sure it had turned its head to follow her. It made her wonder – once she was safely far enough away not to think the bird was chasing her – how many magicians there were around. And why had she not seen that the statues moved when she'd come out before? It hadn't when she was on the way to the fishmonger's yesterday, had it? Or maybe she'd been too busy to notice. Did it only move sometimes? Or perhaps – perhaps only for some people... Bill was so firmly not of the magical world that she was sure he wouldn't see moving statues, like he couldn't feel the stairs move under him. When Rose had been with him, had she seen only what he saw, because she hadn't expected anything else? Now that she was out on her own, with time to look, what other magics might she see? An excited pulse began to beat inside her.

Bill had told her that magic was rare and expensive, and only rich people could pay for it, but there might be the odd bit about, surely? Shut away in St Bridget's, the girls had had no idea about magic and its owners. It was as far away as a fairy tale, and as romantic. But in this real world, perhaps it was more part of things than Rose had realised. Although if the Fountain house servants were anything to go by, everyday people found it frightening, and almost disgusting to see too much of it. Maybe they only wanted to see the pretty side, the grand, exciting bits like the stained-glass windows in the church. They were dramatic, but safe. Mr Fountain's bubble was too easy. He'd probably just snapped his fingers and sent it floating off downstairs, without even having to think. *That* was what had frightened everyone in the kitchen. Magic, just swimming about...

Clearly magic was everywhere at Court, if Mr Fountain was there every day, magicking up gold for the king. Perhaps some of these people she was walking past now were magicians, or magicians' children? She was passing the railings of another park now, full of children, all closely watched by doting parents or servants. A group of small boys was gathered round a fountain, cheering on a toy yacht remarkably like the one she had invented for Maisie. The fountain looked the same, too, a big marble bowl, with a spouting fish in the middle. Rose shivered slightly, and hurried past, not wanting to look. How on earth had she known?

She was into the shopping streets now. Rose crept along by the windows, trying not to get in anyone's way. The girls at the orphanage had admired Miss Bridges' pretty black hat, but her outfit positively dowdy compared to some of the women Rose saw now. She was almost swept into a doorway by one young lady, swishing along in the most enormous black-and-white checked skirt. Rose, having just helped to make herself four dresses, was fairly sure that that skirt could have supplied at least six. The woman saw her staring, and twitched the skirt away irritably, as though she thought Rose might put dirty little fingerprints on it.

If I really do have magic, Rose thought to herself, *one day perhaps I could earn enough money to buy a dress like that. Or bigger even. But even then I wouldn't. She just looks stupid.* It made her feel a lot better. She stuck her tongue out at the woman's back, and someone giggled.

It was a little boy, wearing a very stiff collar, and a rather hot-looking suit. He was with his sister and a nursemaid, standing by the window of the pastrycook's shop. Rose looked at him warily, wondering if he would get her into trouble somehow, but he turned away to tug at his nurse's hand. 'Can we go to the park now?'

'In a minute, Edward. No cake today, Miss Louisa!' The nurse sounded harassed.

'Come on, Lulu,' the boy moaned. 'The park!'

'I want a cake! Mama always lets us have cake! I want a cake now!' The girl, who was at least as old as Rose, she was sure, screamed and stamped, her face turning scarlet under an ostrich-feathered hat, rather like Miss Sparrow's. 'I want that one!'

Rose couldn't help looking, to see what she was making such a fuss about. She was even worse than Isabella, this girl. Even the littlest ones at the orphanage wouldn't have dared behave like this.

But she could almost understand it when she turned to see. The shop window was full of cakes so beautiful that they didn't look real. Cake at the orphanage only happened on incredibly special occasions, and even then it was fruitcake, heavy and dark and long-lasting. The girls had thought it was wonderful, but it was nothing like this. The centrepiece of the window was an enormous three-tiered cake, all crusted in sparkling white icing. Rose guessed it was a wedding cake, although she'd never seen one. The matrons at the orphanage had been much given to reading the newspaper reports of grand society weddings, and they had always had cakes. This one was decorated with sugar flowers, whole pink roses with their petals fashioned from icing, and real primroses, covered in sugar. Rose stared at it – it was so pretty, and so natural. The flowers looked as though they had grown there, the petals waving gently in the breeze. But there wouldn't be a wind in the shop, would there? Rose frowned at the cake. She knew magic was too expensive for everyday things, but perhaps, for a very grand wedding?

The other cakes weren't magical, as far as she could see, but most of them were oozing with cream, or decorated with curls of chocolate. A row of sugar mice near the front of the window sparkled pink, with curly string tails. Rose's mouth watered. She could see why Louisa was making such a fuss, almost. It was somehow more surprising that the little boy didn't seem to care.

Louisa was now hammering on the window with her fists, and screaming, while the nurse tried to tug her away, and her brother slunk closer to Rose. Rose had a feeling he was trying to look as though he belonged with her instead. He stared through the glass at the gingerbread men, as though their chocolate-drop buttons were the most interesting thing he'd ever seen. Rose giggled, imagining them slowly levering themselves off their tray, and prowling amongst the other cakes. They were probably just the right size to ride the sugar mice.

'Did you know,' the little boy asked her, in a tight sort

of voice, as he pretended to ignore his sister, 'that Princess Jane and Princess Charlotte have gingerbread men that move for tea?'

'Really?' Rose looked at him in surprise. Had he read her thoughts? Or was it just that it was impossible to look at the rich gingeriness of those gingerbread men, with their glossy icing swirls, and not imagine them running away?

'My nurse says so. And a magic doll's house, full of fairies. But I think she made that bit up.' He flinched as Louisa screamed like a banshee. 'Oh, I do wish she'd stop,' he muttered.

The pastrycook's window was made of thick, beautifully polished glass, full of darting reflections of the street and the shop staff as they trotted about inside. Rose stared at it thoughtfully. Perhaps she could... It would only be like the pictures, and it would serve Louisa right. It would be such fun. Rose knew inside that she shouldn't, but her fingertips were prickling excitedly, and she just couldn't resist.

'Oink, oink,' she whispered under her breath. Would this still work? Louisa's screaming reflection altered slightly as Rose stared, the red face squashing just a little more, the nose growing...

'Louisa! You're a pig, look!' Edward pointed delightedly and started to crow with laughter.

Louisa clapped her hands across her face, whimpering. She looked like she was about to be sick, but at least she'd stopped screaming. The nurse hustled her off at once, and Edward ran after them, waving at Rose, and beaming. It looked like she'd made his day.

Rose grinned to herself and set off in the same direction. She had better hurry on to St Bridget's now, or she wouldn't have time to see Maisie. Miss Lockwood was sure to want to talk to her first, to check that she was doing the orphanage credit.

It was odd to walk up to the outside of the building alone, not in a crocodile of fifty other girls. Rose hesitated at the door, feeling strangely ashamed of herself as she stood before the place again. She knew they would be delighted to see her – one of the orphanage's success stories – but now she was here, she couldn't hide from herself that she had come to gloat. To see her friends, but also to enjoy telling them about her room, and her dresses, and perhaps, to Maisie only, the strange new skills she was beginning to learn.

She almost turned away – though what would she say to Bill? – but there was an excited scuffling noise behind the door, and it swung open. Ruth and Florence grabbed her delightedly. They were wearing cleaning overalls, so Rose guessed they had been polishing the stained glass in the door and had spotted her. They were two of the oldest girls, and the older ones always fought for the best jobs.

'You're back!' Ruth squeaked. 'Didn't they like you? Was it awful? Did you run away?'

'Don't be silly, she's only visiting,' Florence said contemptuously. 'Aren't you?'

Rose nodded.

'Girls! Did I hear the door open? What's going on out here?' Miss Lockwood came sailing out of her office, her keys jangling from her hand as though she thought someone might be trying to escape.

Ruth bobbed a curtsey. 'It's Rose, Miss!' she said excitedly. 'Come back to visit!'

Miss Lockwood smiled. 'Ah, Rose!' she said graciously. Then her face changed. 'You've not been sent back?' she asked sharply. 'Did you not give satisfaction?'

'Oh, no, Miss, I mean, yes, Miss…' Rose stammered, not helped by Florence imitating her behind Miss Lockwood's back. 'I've a note!' she gasped out, pressing it into Miss Lockwood's hand.

The Governess tore it open anxiously, and read it, muttering. 'Hard-working…polite…frugal habits… This is most excellent, Rose…'

Florence was now trying to use her duster as a halo, and simpering.

Miss Lockwood wheeled round and swatted at

Florence with the note. 'Windows, Florence! Rose, follow me to my office. We will have a cup of tea!'

Rose trotted after her, waving at Ruth and Florence. Tea! It was unheard of for an orphan to have tea with Miss Lockwood. But then, she wasn't officially an orphan now. It was difficult to remember.

She had hardly ever been in Miss Lockwood's office. Certain favoured older girls went in to dust, but otherwise only girls who had Relics to view ever saw it. She'd peeped through the door on a few occasions, and Maisie had told her about the glass-topped tray of sad little mementoes. Rose could see it on the table by the window. She reminded herself to watch out for Miss Lockwood's glass eye.

Miss Lockwood busied herself with a kettle, and a tiny spirit lamp. She chose cups from a little cabinet in the corner – dithering over which ones to use, Rose noticed. Not the gold-rimmed. Rose merited only the flower pattern. All the time she kept up a delighted monologue, saying how pleased she was that Rose was finding her place comfortable, and that the housekeeper had been most complimentary about the orphanage's training. And Rose sat politely on the edge of her chair, hoping for a good moment.

At last she simply interrupted when Miss Lockwood broke off for a minute to pour the tea. 'Might I be allowed to speak to Maisie for a minute, Miss?'

'Maisie?' Miss Lockwood's face was blank. 'Oh, *Maisie*! No, no, I'm sorry, Rose. Maisie has gone.'

Rose simply stared at her. Maisie had gone? Where? 'She – she's not dead, Miss?' Rose had known several girls at the orphanage who had died – there had been an epidemic of scarlet fever the previous year, and though St Bridget's was scrupulously clean, illness spread very quickly with so many children packed together.

'No!' Miss Lockwood shook her head slightly. 'Those terrible flies!' she muttered. 'Buzzing and buzzing.'

Rose couldn't see any flies, but she nodded politely, desperate for Miss Lockwood to go on.

'No, of course she's not dead – no, Rose, Maisie had the most wonderful news. Her mother came for her.' Miss Lockwood's eyes were bright with tears, and she pulled a small lace handkerchief from the hanging pocket at her waist, and blew her nose daintily. 'It was most affecting – the joy as they were reunited after all this time. Maisie's mother, Mrs James, was quite overcome.'

'Her mother?' Rose repeated stupidly. 'Really?'

'I know – it happens so rarely. And a most privileged family, Rose! Quite wealthy! Mrs James came in her own carriage, and just swept little Maisie away!'

Miss Lockwood smiled. Obviously the rediscovery of Maisie had satisfied her romantic imagination perfectly. 'And Maisie remembered her boat!' she added, dabbing another tear.

'Her boat?' Rose asked, a sudden sharpness in her voice.

Miss Lockwood lowered her handkerchief, and blinked. She wafted the lacy scrap about, as though at more flies. 'Yes – Maisie remembered the afternoon she lost her parents. She was sailing a toy boat. So sad. Her mother was in floods of tears as Maisie told her, she hadn't thought she would remember. And Maisie had on her little pink coat, her favourite. Mrs James had to borrow a handkerchief when Maisie told her of it.'

The boat! The boat that Rose had invented – it couldn't be true! She had been certain that she had *made that story up*! And it was true all along? Perhaps she had pulled it out of Maisie's baby memories somehow...

Rose sat staring at the polished floorboards, trying to make sense of it all. She felt that same sense of shame that had gripped her outside the orphanage. *She* had been the one with the exciting news! She had been coming to tell Maisie all the wonderful things that were happening, and now Maisie wasn't even here! She'd gone off and found herself a home! Rose felt absurdly disgruntled. *You're being stupid, and selfish*, she told herself crossly. *Maisie must be so happy.*

'I don't suppose I'll ever see her again,' she murmured.

Miss Lockwood shook her head sympathetically. 'Probably best not, dear. It's a new start for Maisie now. Alberta, I should call her, of course.'

'Alberta?' Rose wanted to giggle. Skinny little Maisie just didn't look like an Alberta. 'Alberta James,' Rose murmured. It sounded real. A real name. She blinked, her eyes strangely hot, and then shook herself crossly. She was getting as sentimental as Miss Lockwood.

The little clock on the mantelpiece chimed, and Rose jumped up. 'Oh, I must go, Miss, I have to be back. Thank you for letting me visit, and giving me the news. Please will you tell the others I was thinking of them?'

'Of course, dear.' Miss Lockwood stood up with a rustle of skirts.

Rose walked round to the door, glancing idly at the strange collection of scraps of paper, little portraits, and assorted tatty jewellery that lay in the glass case.

'Do come back and see us again, Rose,' Miss Lockwood told her graciously as she opened the front door for her.

She was still standing at the top of the steps watching when Rose looked back at the corner of the road. She waved her handkerchief, and then frowned. Clearly the

157

flies were still bothering her. Some of the girls had said that Miss Lockwood kept gin in the little silver milk jug in her office, and Rose had never believed them. But today she certainly had been behaving rather strangely.

Rose walked home slowly, thinking about Maisie. Alberta James. They would grow her hair, and she'd be plump again, like she had been as a little girl in her pink coat. It was hard to imagine it – hard to believe it, either. There was something not right. She could only picture Maisie in the storeroom, the chain of her locket wound round her fingers, staring at it with hungry grey eyes in a greyish face.

Suddenly Rose stopped dead in the middle of the pavement, causing a smartly dressed nursemaid pushing an enormous perambulator to nearly run her over. Rose apologised mechanically and drew to the side of the pavement, her heart thudding with panic.

The little girl in the pink coat. The locket.

Rose *had* invented that coat, because she'd seen it the afternoon she'd told the story – Sunday, only ten days ago, on the girls walking past.

And the locket – she could see it now, dangling from Maisie's hand – *had still been in the cabinet*. Lying there just a few minutes ago, grubby and tarnished, with its broken chain. Maisie wouldn't have left without it, would she? Her most precious possession?

And come to think of it, if Maisie had been accidentally lost, not abandoned, why did she have the locket at all? Rich little girls didn't have that sort of necklace. A string of seed pearls, perhaps, or a gold cross. Real gold. That locket was the sort of gimcrack little thing several of the orphans had, left with them when their mothers brought them to St Bridget's. Mothers who hadn't been able to afford to keep them.

There was something very wrong here.

Maybe Miss Lockwood hadn't been drunk – she'd been lying.

TWELVE

Rose leaned against the park railings, thinking furiously. She was right. She knew it. It *had* been too good to be true. But that wasn't what was important – where was Maisie now? And why would someone go to all that trouble to steal an orphan? Rose clutched at the silly little amulet that Mrs Jones had given her. She kept it in her pocket, like she'd been told, even though she was sure it did nothing. Maisie was another missing child now. Another stolen child.

She hadn't time to think about it properly – she really did need to get back to Mr Fountain's house. But all the time she was hurrying back, scurrying down the area steps, and politely answering Mrs Jones's enquiries about her visit, the questions were turning and fidgeting in the back of her mind.

Freddie appeared suddenly in front of her as she carried the tray back from Miss Isabella's supper. She hadn't eaten most of it, and Rose had had to clean the rice pudding off the nursery wall. She nearly had to clean it off the floor of the corridor too, but Freddie grabbed the tray as it slid from her hands.

'Why do you always have to pop up like that!' Rose snapped. He'd frightened her, and she was jumpy with worry anyway. 'Don't you ever just walk up to people like a normal person?'

Freddie looked hurt. 'I wanted to see you, that's all! There's no need to shout at me. I only wanted to know what you thought of Miss Sparrow, since you had to run off before.' He scowled. 'You're far too rude for a housemaid, you know.'

His cold, grand voice was back again, and Rose realised she'd gone too far. She wasn't sure if it was his feelings that were hurt, or if he was angry that she had stepped out of her place. She hardly cared. She sighed, and rested the edge of the tray on one of the wide windowsills. 'I'm sorry. Something's happened. It wasn't your fault.' Miss Sparrow – it seemed an effort to call the woman back into her mind, too full of Maisie's disappearance. 'You're right, I didn't like her either – she made me shivery.' Rose rubbed her hands over her face wearily. What was she going to *do*?

Freddie took the tray off her, and Rose glanced up at him in surprise. 'You looked like you were about to drop it again,' he explained, putting it on the floor, and sitting down on the windowsill instead. 'Come on, sit down. What's wrong with you? Did you decide you preferred the orphanage?' he asked worriedly. 'Do you want to go back, is that it?'

Rose blinked at him. 'Are you stupid?' she asked sharply, before she could stop herself. 'Of course not!' she continued, more politely. He really had no idea, she supposed. He couldn't help it. Slowly, as she tried to make sense of it herself, she told him about the afternoon, and the Maisie mystery.

'You can make pictures?' He sounded fascinated. 'I've never heard of that before!'

'That isn't what's important now!' Rose reminded him angrily. 'I'm sure Miss Lockwood was lying, she was behaving really strangely, I told you.'

Freddie shook his head. 'I don't think so.'

'But she was! Didn't you understand about the coat? I made that up, that bit of the story! I know for certain I did. So Maisie's mother can't have remembered it. It's all lies, and something awful's happened to Maisie!' Rose wailed.

'I'm not saying it's true, I'm saying Miss Lockwood

wasn't lying! Just listen, can't you? You said you thought she was lying because she kept being strange, and flapping that handkerchief around—'

'Like she was nervous,' Rose put in, nodding. 'So?'

'But she thought there were flies!' Freddie said triumphantly. 'Buzzing round her head. Come on, Rose, don't you see? Something strange going on? Something suspicious? A buzzing noise? It's like I told you earlier! She's been enchanted. Someone's come at her with a glamour. A pretty massive one, too, I should say, if she's still got the side effects now.'

Rose stared at him, her mouth open. She was too used to thinking he was plain silly to admit he was right all at once. 'Someone made her see what wasn't really there,' she murmured.

Freddie nodded smugly. 'Probably they did it to Maisie, too, to make her go with them.'

Rose gulped. 'She would have wanted to believe so badly,' she told him drearily. 'She'd have spilled out that stupid story about the fountain and her toy boat as soon as they walked in the door. I just made it easier for them to take her.'

'Why though?' Freddie asked. 'Why her?'

Rose frowned. 'That's what bothers me. She – she wasn't special. She was my friend, but she was just an orphan.'

Freddie glanced uncomfortably at Rose. 'Maybe that's it. Just an orphan.'

'What are you trying to say?' Rose's voice was small. She had a horrible feeling she knew what he was trying *not* to say.

'Well, no one would miss her, would they?' Freddie looked at the floor. 'The orphanage thinks she's got a new life, and they don't want to remind the new little rich girl who she was. No one else is going to come asking, are they?'

'Except me.' Rose glared at him. 'They didn't know about me, did they?'

'Heaven help them,' Freddie mumbled. Rose ignored him.

'What would anyone want to steal orphans for? Because I bet she isn't the only one! And there are all these other children – Mrs Jones keeps telling me about them, from the newspaper, and there were two in the prayers at church. Two girls.' Rose stood up, her fists clenched. 'I have to find out. I didn't mind never seeing Maisie again when I thought she was going to be Alberta James and have a pony and a doll's house and – and a family! But no one's just going to steal my best friend!'

Freddie blinked. 'Well, quite,' he murmured, rather nervously. 'Umm. What are you going to do?'

'I don't know.' Rose sat down again, looking shrunken. 'I haven't the first idea. Can you think of anything?'

'We could try scrying for her, I suppose…' Freddie said doubtfully. 'I've never done it before, but I know it's in Prendergast, so it ought to be doable. Maybe we could persuade Gus to help. He's good at things to do with seeing – his eyes, you know.'

'You'd really help?' Rose stared at him in amazement. 'Why?'

Freddie gave a helpless sort of shrug. 'I don't know. You saved me from the elemental spirit. I'm obliged.' He frowned. 'I shouldn't be obliged to a servant, and I need to repay the debt.' His shoulders slumped a little, and he didn't look at Rose as he went on quietly, 'And you talk to me. Mostly to be rude, but no one else does at all apart from Gus. Even old Fountain hardly sees I'm here, and when I go home for tea all my parents do is tell me to work harder. If you go off and get stolen too, I'd – I'd miss you!'

Rose glared at him. 'Don't go getting silly!' she warned him firmly.

Freddie shook his head vigorously – his smooth blond hair didn't stir. Rose was more and more convinced that it was stuck to his head with magic. 'I'm not! But I've had months of really only talking to a cat, and Gus can't help seeing things differently. He's a bit mouse-focused.'

'I suppose,' Rose nodded. 'So, what's this scrying thing? Is it like glamours?'

'No, it just means looking for her. I don't know if it'll work, though – I'd have thought someone would have already tried it for those other children. I don't think the police approve of magic, maybe that's why.' Freddie looked around. 'We'd need a glass, or something like that.' He looked thoughtful.

'Like a magic mirror?' Rose asked doubtfully. Half the time she still suspected Freddie of having her on.

'Ye-es, but you don't talk to it, you just look. Or we could use water. Anything shiny. Flames work for some people.'

Rose stared at him. It sounded very like what she'd been doing back at the orphanage, making pictures on shiny things. Maybe she'd be able to do it. 'Can you scry into the past?' she asked slowly.

'Some people can. But it's difficult, and they charge enormous amounts of money for it, so it's not done very often. One of my father's cousins can read the past, and he spends half the year on his estate in Scotland now. Salmon-fishing, and seeing things in rivers.' Freddie smiled dreamily. 'Of course, if you can see into the future, you can just name your price. Hardly anyone can do that.'

Rose shuddered. 'I'd hate it. What if you saw something you didn't want to know?' Then she looked down at the tray and gasped. 'Mrs Jones'll think the stairs have eaten me!' Snatching it up, she scurried down the corridor, glancing back over her shoulder. 'Can you meet me in your workroom tonight?'

If the house was odd in the daytime, after midnight and by candlelight it was positively eerie. Rose edged along the corridor by feel, trying not to imagine what the strangely sticky patches were. The white porcelain of the door handle was a welcome relief. The door slid open noiselessly, and Freddie looked up from the hand mirror he was staring into. The candlelight made his face whiter than ever, with heavy smudged shadows round his black eyes. He looked like a ghost in striped pyjamas. The workroom was dark around the edges, the light only spreading across the big table. The strange apparatus cast flickering shadows, and the liquids gleamed oddly here and there. Rose wrapped her hand protectively round her candle flame. She really didn't want it to go out in here.

'Oh good, we've been waiting ages! I persuaded Gustavus to come, but you have to give him extra cream – you can manage that, can't you?'

Rose smiled smugly, and unfolded a small, rather smelly handkerchief-wrapped parcel. 'Mr Fountain's supper. He didn't eat it all.'

'Crab sandwiches!' Gustavus surged along the table. 'Dear child,' he murmured, in between mouthfuls. 'I would do *anything* for crab sandwiches.'

'Good. Tell us what we ought to use, then,' Freddie demanded. 'I've got a mirror, and this funny old bowl. I've put some water in it, look. Or we can light one of the good candles, if we want. Rose says she's seen things in boots, but I don't think it was proper scrying.'

'That funny old bowl, as you put it, Frederick, is a ritual object, dating back to the time of the druids,' Gus told them, rather thickly. 'I dread to think what they used it for. No more sandwiches, I suppose?' he asked Rose in a hopeful tone. 'Oh, well. Mmm. Try the mirror. It's the easiest way for beginners.'

Rose stared into the mirror, which lay flat on the table. Her hair looked even darker next to Freddie's whiteness. 'What do I do?' she asked him.

'Prendergast says to try to see beyond your own reflection, *into the mists of the otherworld*,' Freddie told her helpfully, consulting the book.

'And what does *that* mean?' Rose asked. 'I don't see any mists, I just see me. Oh!'

'What? Did you see something?' Freddie peered

eagerly over her shoulder.

'It went dark. Was it supposed to do that?' Rose looked closer, her nose almost touching the mirror. 'I can't see Maisie, or anything. Only black.'

'Interesting.' Gus's whiskers tickled the glass as he looked too. 'Try thinking about this girl. Imagine her. Remember the last time you saw her.'

Rose tried. Perhaps she was confusing Maisie as she had really been, with the little girl in the pink coat, and Alberta James who never was, because nothing came into the glass, however hard she thought.

Gus huffed expressively, and his whiskers danced. 'A child surrounded by darkness. I don't like it. You need an artefact. Something of hers to focus on. Like a dog sniffing for a scent. Have you anything?'

Rose shook her head. 'No, nothing.' She tried again to force a picture of Maisie into her mind, but it slipped and shimmered and wouldn't stay. Rose clenched her teeth. Her face was as pale as Freddie's now. The mirror was only dark, but it seemed dangerous. The blackness felt malevolent and cold. And it seethed – like thousands of spiders all squashed together behind the glass. She straightened up at last, abandoning the mirror, and blinking at Freddie and the cat. The candlelight was warm and soft after the icy dark of the glass. 'It's not working. I'll have to go back to the orphanage instead.

There must be some record. Something saying where they took Maisie. Don't you think? A clue?'

They stared back at her doubtfully, and she sighed. 'Well, there's nothing else. I won't just give up.' She brightened a little. 'And I could get the locket! Then we could try this again.' Rose cast a reluctant glance at the mirror. She really didn't want to. 'Maisie loved that locket so – the scrying would be sure to work better then?' Her voice was pleading.

'Perhaps…' Gus nodded.

Rose curled up on a chair, tucking her feet into her nightgown for warmth. The chill of the mirror seemed to be running through her blood. 'I'll go back then, next week.' She bit her lip anxiously. 'A whole week, though!' If that blackness *was* anything to do with Maisie, she didn't want her there a day longer. 'I don't suppose they'll let me take my afternoon off any earlier, will they?' she murmured, half to herself. ''Specially as I can't explain why.'

Gus snorted delicately. 'I should like to see you explaining to Mrs Jones that you've seen your friend in a mirror surrounded by darkness. She'd probably dose you with senna pods. Silly woman doesn't really believe in magic, for all it pays her wages.'

'But what am I going to do? Do you think I might be able to go there when they send me out on an errand?

Maybe if I ran I could get to St Bridget's…'

Freddie shook his head slowly. 'That won't help you, though. You can't just walk in and rifle through the records, can you? And how are you going to explain wanting the locket?'

Rose rubbed her hands over her eyes wearily. He was right.

'You'll have to break in,' Freddie said. His voice was matter-of-fact, but when she looked up in amazement Rose caught an excited gleam in his eyes.

Gus gave a stately nod. 'He's right.'

'Are you both mad?' Rose asked. 'You want me to burgle the orphanage…'

'I shouldn't think it would be very difficult,' Freddie said thoughtfully. 'Aren't they mostly trying to stop people getting *out*?'

'Bars work both ways,' Rose muttered. But he was right. She knew ways they could get in. If they wanted to.

THIRTEEN

Although she hated the idea – what on earth would happen if they were caught? She would be sacked for sure, and probably sent back to the orphanage and locked up there till she was fourteen. Then they'd send her down a mine, or something – Rose couldn't help but agree. It was the only way.

'Drat that Sparrow woman,' Gus said, as they crept along the corridors. 'If it weren't for her, we could ask the master, but when I spoke to him this morning he didn't listen to a word I said. And he did no work this afternoon. Not a scrap of magic. He just stared out of the window, smiling,' he added sadly.

Rose frowned, remembering her first meeting with Mr Fountain, those glinting, all-seeing blue eyes. She couldn't imagine him gazing foolishly out of a window.

'Tomorrow, as soon as Susan is asleep, then,' Freddie warned Rose, as they parted by the servants' stairs.

She nodded, and climbed wearily back up to her room. The work of the house wasn't harder than the orphanage, after all, but she was getting considerably less sleep.

Rose woke to find Susan shaking her roughly.

'Come on, you lazy little brat, wake up! We've the fires to do. Will you get out of bed!'

While she was washing Rose decided that as soon as she'd sorted out Maisie, she would get Freddie and Gus to help her turn Susan into something horrible. Just because she didn't want to tell everyone she could do magic, it didn't mean she couldn't make use of it. Occasionally.

Mrs Jones was reading the newspaper with her morning tea when Rose arrived back from lighting the fires. 'Poor little mite,' she was muttering. 'That poor woman. She must be beside herself.'

'What is it, Mrs Jones?' Rose asked curiously. She knew the cook liked nothing better than to gossip over the news in the mornings. Mrs Jones was particularly fond of the more gory murders, and in the stifling warmth of the basement kitchen, with the gas lamps reflecting off the copper pans, the accounts did resemble some far-off fairy tale.

Mrs Jones peered round the newspaper. 'Another child gone, dear. Another! Don't you go lingering out on the streets when you go on an errand, Rose. It's not safe. Police! Bunch of spineless rabbits. Hah! I don't know what the world's coming to, I really don't.'

Rose slipped round to read over her shoulder.

MYSTERIOUS DISAPPEARANCE IN KENSINGTON
YOUNG GIRL MISSING
POLICE BAFFLED

'They're only bothering now because it's rich kids,' Bill muttered, pouring half a jar of honey onto his porridge. 'Four, they say! More like twenty-four.'

'What are you talking about?' Rose asked. Missing children. More and more of them. Not just Maisie. It all had to be connected, she was sure. There was a cold feeling in her stomach, as though she was staring into that black mirror again.

'Street children. They went first. But no one cares, do they? Tidies the place up a bit, if there's no one sleeping in the shop doorways. The police only took notice when it was the little darlings from round here that started disappearing.' Bill stabbed his porridge angrily, and Mrs Jones rustled her paper.

'Nonsense! Stop frightening Rose. There can't be that many, the police would know.'

But Rose thought she looked rattled – as though she'd like to believe what she was saying, but didn't, quite.

Rose borrowed the paper later that morning when she spotted it lying on the table, but it hardly said anything more – just a heartbreaking description of the lost child's parents, who were offering a large reward for her safe return.

Was it connected to Maisie's disappearance too? It couldn't just be coincidence. She'd laughed to herself when Mrs Jones gave her that funny little bag of herbs, but she should have taken it more seriously. All those children. What could someone want with all those children? Rose shuddered. Freddie was right. They had to get into the orphanage tonight, no waiting, whatever it took. There must be clues there, somewhere, and it might not be just Maisie who needed rescuing.

That is, if they were still alive to be rescued.

'You're kidding me...' Rose whispered angrily.

'No, I'm not! What did you think we were going to do, wander along to the front door and pull back all the bolts in the middle of the night? Perhaps wave to the constable as we stroll down the front steps?' Freddie stood by the open window with his arms folded, and his black eyes snapping with impatience. 'Even doing this we've got to leave Gus behind to talk to the alarm spells for us.'

'Could you please hurry up!' the white cat hissed at them. 'This window *really* wants to shut!' He was sitting on the occasional table, next to another pretty Ming vase. Distractedly, Rose hoped he was being careful. His ears were laid almost flat to his head, and he was staring grimly at the window.

Rose leaned over the windowsill, and looked down into the dark alley that ran along the side of the house. 'But why this window? Why not one of the ground-floor ones?' she wailed.

'Because this one has the wisteria to climb down,' Freddie pointed out, in the over-patient tone of someone talking to the very dim. 'And Gus can't do the downstairs windows. They've got more spells on.'

'I'm not going to be able to do this one for much longer! Will you stop creating and get on!' Was it Rose's imagination, or were the white cat's whiskers starting to fizzle at the ends?

'It's all right for you, you're not wearing a skirt,' Rose moaned, as she looked at the wisteria, laden with purple flowers. It was very *thin*…

'It's stronger than it looks,' Freddie said helpfully.

'I think…' Then he giggled.

'Why are you enjoying this so much? You've got to climb down it too. We could break our necks!' Rose glared at him.

'It's an adventure, isn't it?' Freddie said happily. 'It's like something Jack Jones, Hero of the Seven Seas, would do. He'd be down that wisteria like a shot!'

Rose shook her head sadly. 'He's *drawn* that way, Freddie,' she muttered. 'He probably bleeds ink.'

'Well, if you fall you'll probably bounce,' Freddie said. 'Magic, remember? I fell down the stairs a week or so ago and I floated. It was fantastic.' He stuck his head out of the window. 'Maybe we should just jump! Oh, come on, Rose.' He shook his head at her in a lordly fashion. 'It's only like climbing a tree!'

'I've never climbed a tree! And anyway, I should think you start from the bottom, not the top, which is what's worrying me.' Rose looked down at the dark ground and shuddered.

'Go! Now!' Gustavus gasped. 'It's starting to close. If you don't go right now, you won't go at all!'

Freddie and Rose drew their heads in anxiously and looked up. Gus was right. The sash window was starting to slide slowly but inexorably down.

'I'll go first, then I can catch you if you fall,' Freddie said gallantly.

177

'You most certainly won't!' Rose stuck one leg over the windowsill. She had been well trained at St Bridget's and she was allowing no one the chance to peep up her skirt. 'Oh my goodness,' she murmured, as the wisteria wobbled under her. A waft of sweet scent billowed around as she shook the flowers.

'Hurry!' Freddie was hanging out of the window. 'It's shutting faster now, I'm going to have to come after you!'

Rose felt the wisteria stems shake as Freddie climbed out onto them. *Don't fall off the wall, don't fall off the wall,* she begged it, as she clung on tighter, feeling with her foot for the next sturdy branch. In her haste to be on the ground before Freddie's extra weight made the whole thing collapse, one foot slipped, and she slid downwards, grabbing frantically at the branches. *Help!*

'Rose, are you all right?' Freddie hissed.

'I think so,' Rose gasped back. Miraculously she seemed to have kept her hold, and she was only a few inches from the ground now. 'But I'm not sure I can move. It's – um – it's holding on to me.'

'What is?' Freddie was almost level with her now. He was obviously a practised climber, and he landed on the paving slabs with a gentle thump and a smug grin which made Rose want to smack him. She held out her wrist. 'Look.'

'Oh…' Freddie's grin faded. 'Er, did you ask it to do that?'

Rose looked at the leafy, bright-green stems that were wrapped round her arm. 'I might have done,' she agreed cautiously. 'I did think *Help!* when I was slipping.'

'Mmmm. And it did. Maybe you should tell it you're all right and it can let go?' Freddie suggested.

Rose stared pleadingly at the wisteria. 'Um, thank you…' she whispered.

'Do you have any other amazing magical abilities you'd like to tell me about now, before we go any further? You know, just in case we need to tame a sea serpent or something, so I don't go risking life and limb unnecessarily?'

Rose shook her head. 'I don't know,' she said, as the wisteria stems gently released her. 'Oh! The statue in the square moved when I looked at it, or at least I thought it did…'

Freddie sniffed. 'It does that for everyone. That's my grandfather, he was horrible when he was alive, and he hasn't changed. Come on.'

Rose trotted after him down the alleyway. 'Do you mean that actually *is* him? I thought it was a statue!'

'Him with a stone coating.' Freddie pulled a tiny lantern out of his pocket, and blew it alight. 'He

179

thought being buried would be boring. He was that sort of person. He once fed me a marble and told me it was a special kind of gobstopper. I nearly choked to death.'

They peered out into the square. It was very dark. The idea of an almost-alive statue watching them from the garden was most off-putting, Rose thought.

'I wish we could run,' she murmured. 'I hate this creeping along.'

'We mustn't. If anyone saw us they'd think we'd done something wrong, and we haven't. Yet.' Freddie lifted his lantern to peer at a street sign. 'If anyone stops us, your mother's ill, and I've come to fetch you home, all right?'

'Yes, I suppose so.' It was odd to think about having a mother, even if it were only an imaginary one. Rose found herself wondering what was the matter with her, and hoping it wasn't anything very serious. 'Round this next corner, we're nearly there.'

The orphanage was tightly barred and shuttered, but all the orphans knew there was a way into Miss Lockwood's garden. Some of the girls still had brothers and sisters outside, who weren't allowed to visit. A few of the local children had loosened some of the bricks and now it was possible to climb the wall into the garden, especially if you had someone to help you up.

Freddie boosted Rose to the top of the wall, and she hauled him up after her.

'Just mind the rose bush as you drop down,' she warned him. 'It's prickly. And I was named after it.'

Freddie gave her a look that Rose suspected was meaningful. 'They aren't connected!' she whispered crossly, as she padded across the tiny square of grass to the window.

'Is it locked?' he called quietly after her, trying to extricate himself from the rose thorns.

'Only latched, I think.' Rose pulled out a butter knife from the pocket of her thick hooded cloak. She had borrowed it from the kitchen, and she had a horrible feeling it was silver – certainly Bill had been polishing it. If she was caught with it outside the house, she would probably be hanged. But it had been all she was able to find. She levered it in between the window and the frame, and pushed the catch up. The window jolted open, and Freddie hurried to shove her in.

'Lucky you're so skinny,' he muttered. 'I can't fit in there. Do you see anything useful?'

Rose looked round, rubbing her bruised side. A few more weeks of living at the Fountain house, and she might not have been able to fit in either. She could see why burglars started young.

Miss Lockwood kept all the children's records in

a big old chest full of narrow drawers. She obviously had some sort of system, but Rose wasn't sure quite what it was, so she just had to ferret through all the drawers.

'Haven't you found anything yet?' Freddie hissed from the window. He was obviously getting twitchy.

'No...' Rose was at the bottom drawer now – it had to be this one. 'Oh, look, this is my record!' Rose's fingers shook a little as she unfolded the form, but it didn't tell her anything new. *Female child found abandoned in St John's churchyard. Aged about one year. Medically sound. Clothing destroyed due to infestation. Christened Rose.* Well. That was it. Except that Miss Lockwood had added last Monday's date and *Placed in service*, alongside the address of the Fountain house.

Rose stuffed it back anyhow, blinking suddenly sore eyes. *Clothing destroyed due to infestation.* Her clothes hadn't even been good enough for an orphanage.

Behind her records was another set, with the name crossed out and rewritten, and behind those were several more like it.

'I've found Maisie's papers!' Rose whispered excitedly to Freddie. 'Alberta James, she's down as now.' She flicked anxiously through the other papers. 'Freddie, look. It isn't just Maisie. There are others too – Lily, and Ellen, and Sarah-Jane... I think Miss Lockwood just puts all the records she's looked at recently together. Four girls all gone from the orphanage in the same week? That's – that's just stupid. No one would ever believe that...'

'Unless they've been glamoured,' Freddie argued.

'But all the other girls would know,' Rose pointed out. 'They can't have bewitched everybody, can they?'

'Depends how good they are,' said Freddie, shrugging. 'Does it say where they've gone?'

'No, just *Found by her family* on Maisie's.' Rose glanced over the others. 'And these are the same. No addresses. You'd think they'd keep an address, wouldn't you?' Rose nibbled the side of a nail, pulling at the skin. 'Lily's only four, Freddie...'

Freddie sighed. 'Get the locket, Rose. There's nothing else, is there?'

Rose crept back to the glass case by the window. Maisie's locket was in one corner, resting on the faded purple velvet lining. Rose knew even more certainly that she would never have left it behind. Even with its chain broken, it had been unbelievably precious to her. If anything could lead them to Maisie, it would be this.

Rose clutched the locket tightly. She could feel the scratched pattern on the metal digging into her fingers, and it felt like she would have flowers engraved on them for ever by the time they reached home. But the locket reminded her of Maisie *so* clearly – she was sure that if only they could stop for a moment, she could scry for her now in its tarnished silvery surface, and not need a mirror at all.

'Hurry up!' Freddie urged, grabbing her hand and pulling her along.

'What's the matter?' Rose murmured vaguely. She was still dazed from knowing that those other girls she'd known were lost too. Little Lily – the last time Rose had seen her she'd been upside down in a washing basket, hysterical with giggles at the excitement of Miss Bridges visiting. And then just a few days later, someone had stolen her away, and she'd become part of a strange, diabolical plot. Rose was wandering through the black streets of a dream world.

'Wake up, Rose!' Freddie shook her arm.

Rose blinked at him crossly. Couldn't he see that she was thinking about important things?

'There's someone following us...' Freddie hissed. 'No, don't turn round! We aren't that far from home, and we can make a run for it once we get into the square. I shouldn't think they'll follow us there. Just walk fast and pretend we haven't noticed! I made a mistake using this lantern, people can tell it's magical. I bet that's what they're after. They think we've got stuff worth stealing.'

Now that she knew they were there, Rose could hear the pattering footsteps, and the whispery breathing behind them. It sounded horribly close. They walked on a few more steps, then all of a sudden Rose couldn't bear it any longer. The hoarse-voiced whispers seemed to be breathing down her neck. She whirled round, pulling Freddie with her, and holding up the locket as if it were some kind of weapon – a fragile shield.

'What do you want?' she screamed, and the ragged group of children shadowing them stopped a few feet away.

'You're not taking us!' a little girl around Isabella's age shrilled at them. 'We'll get you first!' She was shaking with fear and determination, her eyes huge and bright in her dirty little face, and her fingers curled into angry claws.

'Shut up, Sal!' An older boy stepped forward protectively, holding out a knife. His little brother – their faces were so alike, he had to be – followed. He was armed only with a stick, but he looked desperate enough to use it.

'Where's our sister? What have you done with her, you monsters!' the older boy growled. 'You take us to her now, or I'll cut you to ribbons!'

'What are you talking about?' Freddie snarled disgustedly. 'Get away from us!'

Rose glanced at Freddie, shocked at the coldness in his voice. She'd hated him at first, but she'd grown used to his airs, and for the past few days she'd been thinking of him as a friend, or at least as an ally. Now all at once she saw him as the street children did – his shirt shining white in the lantern light, a perfectly fitted suit, neatly tied bowtie. Only the knees of his breeches were grubby from hauling himself up and down walls. He was from another world.

She smiled apologetically at the older boy, but the naked fear and distrust in his face stabbed into her, far harder than the knife still shaking in his outstretched hand ever could. She was with Freddie. She *looked* like Freddie – clean, prosperous, far better fed than these poor castaways. The smile vanished from her face.

'I'll do it! I will!' the boy's voice was higher now as he stepped forward, squeaky with fright.

'And I will too!' the little girl rushed forwards at Rose. 'Give her back! She's only a baby!'

Freddie tried to push Rose behind him into the safety of a doorway, but she shook him off as the tiny girl clawed at her arm and tried to bite her. 'Stop it! Freddie, help me hold her, she's biting me!'

The two boys circled round them, their faces desperate. 'Give her back and we'll let you go! We won't let you take Sal too!'

'What makes you think we want her?' Freddie said contemptuously, gripping the skinny child's wrist, and holding her away as though he couldn't bear to touch her.

Sal was so thin it was like holding sticks that wriggled. 'Keep still!' Rose told her. 'You've got it wrong! Will you stop doing that? Ow!' Rose lost her temper as the child managed to bite her hand at last. 'We don't know anything about your sister, and we don't want this one either!' She flung Sal back towards the boys, not being particularly careful. 'You drew blood, you little weasel!'

Sal scrambled up and spat at her.

'I've had enough of this!' Freddie snapped. 'Dirty little guttersnipe!' And he threw the lantern at the ground where it shattered and flared into a protective wall of greenish flames across the doorway.

'You didn't tell me you could do that!' Rose said admiringly.

'Yes, well, you never said you could talk to trees. You lot, back off! Go on, leave us alone, or we'll set it on you!' he hissed.

The children drew back, their faces pinched with fear, but they didn't run.

'That proves it, it's them, it has to be,' the older boy told his brother. 'You take Sal back. I'm not giving up. You hear that?' he yelled at Rose and Freddie. 'I'm not

187

going, whatever you do. You've got to put that fire out to move, so I'll wait.'

Freddie looked at the flames, and Rose nudged him. 'He's right, you know. It looks good, but we can't get past it either...'

'Actually it doesn't really burn, but I don't want them knowing that. I thought they'd just run away,' Freddie muttered back. 'Why aren't they running? I'd run...'

'They've got something more important to worry about. Hey, when did your sister go missing?' she called to the boy.

'You know!' he yelled back. 'You took her, murderers!'

'You've got it all wrong. They took my friend. We're trying to find them too!' Rose came closer to the flames, trying to see their faces. 'They took Maisie from St Bridget's, the orphanage. You followed us from there, didn't you?'

The boy lowered his knife, very slightly. 'They aren't taking ones like you...' he said doubtfully.

'What do you think I am?' Rose asked. 'I'm a housemaid, I came from St Bridget's, I'm not *like* anything!'

'What about him?' The boy waved the knife at Freddie.

'He's from the house where I work. He's helping me, I promise!'

'She had magic, the one who took Annie,' the little girl said defensively. 'I saw!'

'You've seen who's taking them?' Rose gasped, and stepped through the fire-wall without thinking. The children backed away, gaping, as the flames licked around Rose's boots.

'Wonderful, now they know it doesn't burn,' Freddie said, following her, and dousing the flames with a wave of his hand. 'I can do other stuff, you know,' he threatened, pointing menacingly at Sal.

'Freddie, don't! They've seen her, listen! What did she look like?' Rose begged. 'Someone's taken four girls from the orphanage, pretending they were family. And it's been in the papers, children stolen from the park, and even one from her own bedroom. There'll be more, I know there will. You have to tell us!'

Sal's older brother was looking at them suspiciously, but he'd at least stopped brandishing the knife. 'She was a magician,' he said slowly. 'That's why we thought you were part of it. Going about in the middle of the night, waving that unnatural light around.'

'She told us she was just borrowing Annie!' Sal put in. 'Taking her for a treat, she said. We weren't to worry.'

The boy shook his head. 'And we believed her. I don't know why. It seemed to make sense, until we woke up under the bridge the next morning, and we

189

couldn't understand why Annie wasn't there. Only Sal remembers properly.'

'She was beautiful.' Sal nodded importantly. 'And tall. And she had green eyes that glittered.'

'She must have not bothered with the glamour carefully enough,' Freddie said.

'Maybe she didn't think she needed to...' Somehow that made Rose feel angrier than anything – that the kidnapper hadn't even bothered to deceive these children properly, because she didn't think they mattered.

'Can you help us get her back?' the oldest boy asked gruffly.

'Yes,' Rose told him. 'There can't be two lots of people stealing children, can there? So when we find Maisie, we're bound to find your Annie too. We've got a plan.'

'Which *might* work,' Freddie put in, but Rose elbowed him. 'It will! It's got to,' she added grimly. 'But I can feel it will, like the locket's trying to tell me where Maisie is. I know we can find them.' Looking at Sal and her brothers' desperate faces was like seeing her own fear.

The locket had to work.

FOURTEEN

'It's still just dark!' Rose hit the table angrily, then winced, sucking the side of her hand. 'Oww.'

'There's no point losing your temper with it,' Gus told her in an annoyingly calm voice.

Rose whirled round, still holding the mirror, and nearly swept him off the table. He didn't flinch, but his ears and whiskers flew back as if he was in a strong wind, and he looked up at her warily.

'Don't! Just – don't!' she snarled. 'Smug know-it-all cats are not what I need right now. Find a spell or something, we have to *make* this work. We don't have much more time. If Susan goes to wake me and I'm not in bed, I'll probably be dismissed.' Rose sighed. 'I'm sorry, Gus. I know you're tired too, working the spells

191

on the windows for us. But you didn't see those children tonight, and you don't know Maisie. I can't be calm, I'm not calm! I'm frightened!'

Gus dug his claws in and out of the tabletop, thoughtfully. 'Have you considered that the darkness might be right?'

'What do you mean?' Rose stared at him, and Freddie looked up from Prendergast where he was rereading the scrying instructions again, in case they'd missed something the other seventeen times.

'We-ell, perhaps Maisie is in a dark place...' Gus glanced nervously at Rose, his shoulders slightly hunched, as though he expected she might throw something at him.

Rose sat down suddenly, as though her legs had been taken out from under her. Luckily she'd been next to a chair. 'You mean, we've done it right, but this is all we're going to get? Even with the locket? That can't be it, Gus, we need more!'

'Perhaps we're searching for the wrong thing.' Freddie laid the book down, and came over to stare into the mirror. 'We've been trying to find *where* Maisie is. Maybe we need to look for something else.'

'Like what?' Rose's voice was doubtful. *Where* was what they needed right now.

'Umm, like who took her? Could you look for that?

Maisie might know, and if we find out who the kidnappers are, it could lead us to all the children.'

'We already know there's a lady magician involved,' Rose agreed. 'Sal saw her. We can try, I suppose.'

'And this time try putting the locket on, instead of just holding it,' Gus suggested. 'It might help.'

Freddie helped her tie the broken chain around her neck. The locket felt warm, and almost alive. Like a little bit of Maisie. The thought made Rose smile, and she stared down into the mirror with new hope.

'Who stole you, Maisie?' Rose murmured out loud, without even realising what she was doing. The locket seemed to flutter on her chest, like a tiny bird, and a face suddenly appeared in the mirror.

Rose screamed with shock, and flung the mirror across the table. She felt as though a spider had just walked across her hand.

The face was Miss Sparrow.

The mirror had cracked right across its surface, but the face had stayed, covered now with a sickening web of fine lines. Rose could hardly look at it. It made her skin crawl.

Freddie and Gus crouched next to the mirror where it lay on the floor – no one wanted to pick it up.

'I knew I didn't like her, but I didn't think she

193

was a kidnapper,' Freddie murmured.

'Is it – reliable?' Rose asked, her voice shaking slightly.

Gus nodded, still staring at the face. 'I think so. It was a clear question, and we can't deny the answer.' He shook his whiskers irritably. 'Even in a glass, her face captures you. It isn't just a glamour, it can't be.'

'Have you ever been to her house? With Mr Fountain?' Rose asked, edging back round the table so she didn't have to look at the mirror again.

Freddie shook his head. 'No. He visited her last week, but he didn't take me. That's when he first met her, but she'd been corresponding with him for a while before that. It was something to do with his gold spells, but of course they're secret. She wanted to use one of them for something else. He said she was brilliant, she had ideas no one had ever thought of before. I think he was a bit worried too, at first. Some of the ideas were very strange. But – after he met her...' Freddie shrugged, turning away from the face in the mirror. 'Anyway, I don't know where she lives, but I get the feeling it isn't far from here. He definitely didn't take the carriage.'

Rose gave a huge, sudden yawn that made her jaw crack. 'Ohhh, I'm so tired... Freddie, what are we going to do with – that?' She nodded towards the mirror. Gus was still leaning over it, fascinated. His whiskers were trailing perilously close to the surface, and he suddenly jumped as though he'd been stung.

'Powerful magic,' he muttered, shaking his ears like a cat who'd been caught in the rain. 'Strong stuff. Intoxicating, almost...' He sounded regretful, and Freddie and Rose stared at him reproachfully.

Gus sighed. 'I know, I know, but Fountain hasn't done any exciting new magic for days – more than a week I've gone without it. There's just such a good smell about real magic. I want to know what she's been doing.'

'So do I,' Rose whispered. 'And I don't think it smells good at all – what's that!' She jumped up, pointing. There'd been a scuffling sort of noise outside the workroom door, and now the handle was slowly turning.

Everyone in the house was asleep, or should have been – it was four o'clock in the morning. Somehow, knowing that made the simple turning of a white door handle one of the most terrifying things Rose had ever seen. She backed into the table, her breath tight in her chest.

Freddie picked up the mirror, wincing as though it were hot, and held it behind his back. Gus jumped onto the table, standing protectively between them.

When the door slowly opened to reveal Isabella in

her nightgown, clutching an oversized doll, everyone felt rather foolish.

Then Isabella smiled, sweetly, and Rose began to wonder if they hadn't been so foolish after all. Isabella closed the door behind her, and leaned on it gently, smiling round at them all. She looked remarkably like her doll, with the same golden curls and an identical perfect pink-and-white face.

'You aren't supposed to be here,' Isabella pointed out, still smiling.

'No more are you,' Freddie retorted stoutly, but Rose noticed he was glancing sideways round the room, looking for some sort of rescue, as if it were going to come creeping out of the walls.

'But you woke me up!' Isabella said innocently, opening her big, blue eyes wide. 'You frightened me! All that banging and chattering on the wall outside my bedroom. I thought it was *burglars*!'

'Nonsense! If you'd really thought it was burglars you'd have screamed like a banshee and stuck your head under the pillow,' Gus told her. He looked unimpressed.

'It was her bedroom we were climbing past?' Rose whispered to Freddie. They'd had to call to Gus to let them back in. Rose had tried politely asking the wisteria if it could knock on one of the first-floor windows for them, but it had ignored her. Obviously it did emergencies only. From the way the leaves shuddered, Rose wondered if she'd been rather rude asking. She'd apologised.

They hadn't been very quiet climbing back up, Rose thought to herself. They'd made it home safely, and they were triumphant and jumpy and nervous about trying to scry again. It was no wonder they'd been heard.

Freddie nodded. 'I suppose.'

'You could be dismissed, you know,' Isabella pointed out to Rose, in the most friendly fashion.

Rose eyed her, trying to work out what she wanted. 'Yes,' she agreed. It seemed to take the wind out of Isabella's sails slightly, but only for a moment.

'You're having an immoral tryst,' she reminded Rose, as though she thought Rose ought to be rather more worried about it.

'I most certainly am not! Miss,' Rose added at the last minute. She'd got used to not calling Freddie 'Sir', and to thinking of him as someone she could actually talk to. It made it hard to remember that she was supposed to fawn over Isabella.

'We aren't!' Freddie agreed disgustedly. 'Don't be such a little prude, Bella. Anyway, you aren't really so innocent, you're just pretending to be mealy-mouthed to scare Rose.'

Isabella stared at the ceiling, and said in a rather sing-song voice, 'But I could tell. All I'd have to do is scream, and *everyone* would come running. Then you'd all be in awful trouble, wouldn't you?'

Freddie sighed. 'All right. What do you want?'

Isabella beamed at him. 'I want to know what you're doing,' she told him simply. 'Where did you go?'

Freddie looked apologetically at Rose. 'We'll have to tell her. She's the most terrible little actress, and she's got no conscience whatsoever. She *would* get you dismissed, if she felt like it.'

Isabella didn't seem to mind being talked about like this. She looked smug. 'It's quite true,' she told Rose proudly. 'I've seen off the last two governesses, and I wouldn't give Miss Anstruther more than a couple of weeks. I'm aiming for nervous prostration with her, for variety.'

It was hard to believe Isabella was only seven. She sounded like an accomplished conspirator. Rose began to wonder if she might be rather useful to have on their side. 'We're trying to rescue a friend,' she told the younger girl carefully, wondering how much she ought to let her know. 'Lots of people, actually, but only one that we really know. Her name's Maisie.'

Isabella sniffed rather dismissively. She obviously wanted more details.

'They've been kidnapped. By – by a lady magician.' Rose wasn't sure what to say about Miss Sparrow. She didn't think Isabella would believe them. Mr Fountain was so enamoured that marriage was beginning to be rumoured in the kitchen, so presumably she'd been introduced. But the little girl's head snapped up, and she stared at Rose.

'Who?'

'The Sparrow woman.' Freddie passed the mirror gingerly to Isabella, who dropped her doll and snatched it eagerly. 'That's horrid,' she whispered, entranced. 'I knew there was something wrong about her, I knew!' Surprisingly, when she looked up, her face was gleeful. 'She wants to marry my papa, and I shan't let her! I knew she wasn't good for him, and now no one can say I'm just being selfish, like Miss Anstruther did, not if she's a kidnapper.' Isabella's eyes seemed to harden to glinting jewels. It struck Rose that Miss Anstruther would be lucky to last another two weeks. Her comments had clearly stuck, and Isabella wriggled irritably as if to shake them off.

Freddie sighed. 'Who knows how we're going to stop her, though. She's – well, she's very good. And we're not. To be honest.'

'I am.' Isabella beamed at him. 'And I'm quite ruthless, everyone says so.'

'But what are we going to do?' Rose tried hard not to let a whine creep into her voice, but she was tired, and her legs ached from climbing, and she just couldn't think what should happen next.

Isabella glanced at her contemptuously. 'Servants have no initiative. Or moral fibre.'

Rose felt a surge of anger rush round her body. It did very well at waking her up. 'I've only been a servant for a week and a half, Miss. I've got some fibre left,' she said. Then she wished she hadn't. Isabella was so spoilt, all the servants said so. *No one* answered her back, not even her father, who thought she was an angel. She'd probably have a screaming tantrum now and wake the whole house. Rose gave Freddie a panicked glance, and he rolled his eyes at her. He'd automatically hunched his shoulders as though he was preparing himself for a storm to blow over his head.

Isabella looked at her interestedly, her cheeks slightly flushed. Perhaps she was considering a tantrum – Rose had the feeling that Isabella did very little that wasn't carefully thought through. But she appeared to decide against it. 'Don't you *care* that I could get you dismissed?' she asked Rose, coming to stand near the table. Without even bothering to look at him, she held out her arms to Freddie, and obediently he picked her up. Holding her at arm's length as though she smelled, he sat her on the table, from where she could look down at them all.

Gus moved to the other end, quite fast, and Rose wondered if Isabella had pulled his tail, from the way he wrapped it round him so carefully. It almost seemed to have stretched. Surely it hadn't been long enough before for the end to tuck right under his paws like that?

Isabella surveyed them, like a princess and her courtiers. Then she settled on Rose. 'You aren't just a kitchen-girl,' she said accusingly.

'I'm an under-housemaid, Miss,' Rose said, though she knew perfectly well what Isabella meant.

'Don't play stupid,' Isabella sighed, sounding at least three times her age. 'You aren't that either.'

'She's better at magic than I am.' Freddie had grown tired of the fencing. 'But she's an orphan, Bella. Her parents left her in a fishbasket!' He still sounded as though he couldn't understand the contradiction. Rose supposed it just wasn't how things happened. Magicians bred more magicians. But they must have started somewhere...

'How very odd.' Isabella looked Rose up and down even more thoughtfully. 'I dislike fish.'

'So do I, Miss.' Rose stared back. Isabella seemed to have got past the sacking stage, and Rose thought she rather enjoyed having someone fighting back for once.

Isabella nodded. She was silent for a moment, then she stated firmly, 'I want to help.'

'You can't. If we get you lost, your father will – well, I don't want to think what he'll do.' Freddie exchanged a nervous glance with Gus, whose ears went flat again. They were the ones who knew just what Mr Fountain *could* do. Rose didn't want to think. Especially as it was likely that Miss Sparrow could do it as well.

What was even more frightening was that possibly Rose could, too. That made her feel sick.

202

FIFTEEN

'So how are we going to trap Miss Sparrow?' Isabella asked in a bloodthirsty tone.

'I don't see how we can…' Freddie said doubtfully.

Rose eyed Isabella thoughtfully. 'When we met those children earlier on,' she said to Freddie, 'the girl said that a lady magician came and took their little sister. So she's actually stealing the children herself. If we could just catch her doing it—'

'And then what?' Gus broke in.

'Well, we could follow her,' Rose suggested. 'And then we'd know where she's taking the children, and we could rescue them.'

Gus and Freddie stared dubiously at her, but Isabella

nodded eagerly. 'Of course we could!'

Rose sighed. 'But we don't know where she'll be. I think you're right, Freddie, she must live round here somewhere. The orphanage is close, and so are the places where those children were stolen. The beggar-children too, I think. But we can't watch the whole neighbourhood, that's just silly.'

Isabella kicked her feet excitedly, for once betraying how young she really was. 'It's like I said, you need to trap her. What you need,' – she stared brightly round at them all – 'is bait.' She put on her most innocent, helpless face. It reminded Rose of a man-eating tropical river-fish that she had read about at St Bridget's, in a book called *Lives of the Foreign Missionaries*. Actually, it was mostly deaths.

Gus understood first – he had, after all, the most experience of Isabella. 'No.'

Freddie shook his head vigorously. 'Absolutely not, Bella!'

Rose took a slow, deep breath. 'You can't,' she muttered, but rather admiringly. Isabella was brave, she had to admit.

'So you tell me how else you're going to do it.' Isabella folded her arms, waiting.

Rose took a deep, shaky breath. 'I'll be the bait,' she said quietly. She didn't want to be. The thought of deliberately allowing Miss Sparrow to catch her, for whatever awful scheme she'd devised, made her heart jump and thud in her chest as though it were trying to beat its way out. But she didn't have a choice – that woman already had Maisie, and Lily, and Annie, and all those others. It was the obvious plan.

'You can't!' Isabella's postponed tantrum was clearly going to happen now instead. 'It was *my* idea! Mine, mine, mine!' And she slid down from the table to run at Rose, until Freddie seized her and put his hand over her mouth to stifle her screams. Gus leaped onto his shoulder, and then put his front paws gingerly on Isabella's thrashing arm. Her nails were growing into claws, Rose noticed, shuddering.

'Stop it, you silly, ill-mannered little girl!' the cat hissed, nose to nose with her.

Isabella's eyes widened above Freddie's hand, and she grew scarlet with indignation.

'And don't tell me that your father will have me stuffed. I've been with him since before you were even thought of. If Freddie lets you go, will you be silent for a moment and listen?'

Isabella nodded resentfully, and Freddie released her, jumping back a step. Gus sprang back to the table and Isabella stood there looking like a trapped animal, her hands still raised to show the claws.

'Little beast,' Gus said conversationally, and Isabella snarled.

'Well, quite.' Gus closed his eyes momentarily in disgust. 'She can look after herself, you know,' he pointed out to Rose and Freddie. 'I think we should let her do it. It's the only plan that I can see having even a chance of working. She's too young to have any real power, so Miss Sparrow won't spot her for what she is.'

'But didn't you meet her, when she came to lunch?' Rose asked Isabella. 'I went back to the kitchens after I'd cleaned up the mess you made, so I didn't see. She's not going to kidnap a child she knows, is she?'

Freddie laughed. 'Mr Fountain went to fetch Bella to introduce her to her future step-mama, but Isabella felt differently. A policeman actually called, because someone across the square thought there was a murder being done.'

Isabella shook her pretty curls. 'I won't have her as a mother,' she hissed, and this time Rose was watching for the nails. They were actually growing into Isabella's own palms, and she hadn't noticed. 'And I won't be polite to her, and drink tea. She shan't marry him.'

'Stop it!' Rose cried, pulling at the little girl's hands. 'You're bleeding!'

Isabella blinked, and looked down at her soft pink palms, marked with bloody half-moons. She glanced up at Rose in sudden dismay, and gulped tears. It was the first time she'd been at all like any other little girl Rose had known.

'She won't, all right? I promise. Just don't do that again.'

Isabella nodded, shaking the lace ruffles of her nightgown down over her hands, as though she didn't want to see what she'd done. She leaned against Rose for a moment, and Rose looked down at her in surprise. The touch lasted only seconds, but she could feel that Isabella needed it very much. She hadn't felt sorry for her before – why would she? But now she couldn't help pitying the smaller girl. In a way, she seemed more alone than Rose herself.

That morning, Rose felt as though she had thick soup flowing sluggishly through her veins instead of blood. The two hours' sleep she'd got had made her feel worse, not better. She kept dropping things, as though her fingers didn't belong to her any more, and when she kneeled down to lay Mr Fountain's fire, she woke up who-knew-how-many minutes later to find him standing above her, resplendent in a paisley dressing gown and scarlet Turkish slippers with long pointed toes. The slippers had been next to her cheek as she lay pillowed on her apron, and she hadn't been able to work out what they were, these strange red tasselled things…until she looked up, and stumbled backwards on her knees in a stammering panic.

'Are we working you too hard, child?' Mr Fountain murmured, in a soft, amused voice.

Even through her fear, Rose couldn't help a dart of pity. How awful to be in love with someone like Miss Sparrow! He seemed so completely happy, waving away her apologies, and seating himself in a large armchair by the window, with an almost equally large book spread across his knees. But he didn't read it. He just gazed out of the window at the street, humming to himself.

Rose finished the fire – taking at least six lucifer matches to light it, a dreadful waste – and scurried out of the room.

Having Isabella as a co-conspirator did make things slightly easier. She came back from her morning walk with Miss Anstruther and angelically requested that Susan send Rose to the schoolroom, as she needed help cleaning and relabelling her beetle collection. (Miss Anstruther, apparently, did not do beetles, and was going to lie down.)

Whatever Miss Isabella wanted tended to get done, so Rose gladly took off her apron and left Bill to polish the shoes by himself. He grumpily volunteered to introduce Isabella to some black beetles in the scullery copper, but Rose thought they might be too common for collecting.

'At last!' Isabella grabbed her as she opened the door, hauling her inside. 'I've been waiting *ages.*'

Freddie and Gus were sitting on the window seat. Freddie was yawning and Gus was asleep on his lap.

'Help me get the beetles down,' Isabella demanded, standing on a chair in front of an enormous cupboard crammed full of toys and games.

'But why do we need them?' Rose took the slim wooden case that Isabella was handing down to her and shuddered. 'Urrgh!' They weren't as bad as spiders, but she wasn't fond of beetles either.

'Someone's bound to come in,' Isabella complained, hopping off the chair in a flurry of frilly petticoats. 'They're *always* checking up on me. So you're helping me clean the beetles, and Freddie has brought a beetle book, because I can't identify that one.' She pointed to a large, shiny, black and red-spotted creature with fearsome horns.

'Can't you...' Rose murmured, unconsciously wiping her hands on her skirt as she backed away from the tray.

Isabella sighed impatiently. 'Well, of course I can, silly! It's a handsome fungus beetle. *Mycetina*

perpulchra. From the Americas. But Miss Anstruther doesn't know that, does she? Not if I take the label off. And the maids all squeal like you almost did. So have a duster, and Freddie, come here and open that book, and try to look puzzled just like you usually do, and if anyone comes in we'll be fine.' She flounced down in her chair, and folded her hands in a business like fashion. 'Gus! Don't eat the beetles. So! Where are we going to set the trap?'

Rose gaped at her. She supposed that it was partly due to natural talent, and partly upbringing, and partly having had considerably more sleep, but Isabella seemed so *keen.* And organised. She had scrambled up again for a pencil and paper, and was busily writing a list of possible places.

'The park? Do you think? Or is it too obvious?'

Rose woke up slightly. 'I think one of the other children was taken when he was supposed to be walking home through the park. The newspaper said. So she might go there again…'

'Good!' Isabella nodded happily. 'I shall pretend to be lost, and then she can take me back to her house. Then I'll escape, and free everyone else, and I shall be a heroine.'

'Wonderful,' Freddie muttered. 'So glad you've got it all planned. I'm going back to bed.'

'I might need a *little* help,' Isabella conceded.

'Freddie and I can follow you, then when we know where she's hidden everyone, we can rescue you.' Rose was not allowing herself to admit that it was possible Miss Sparrow hadn't hidden the children. That she hadn't needed to. As the tally of stolen children grew, it seemed increasingly likely that the awful cold blackness in the mirror meant death. She shook her head. 'Isabella – Miss, I mean – would your governess let you go out alone with Freddie? Without her?'

'If she were suitably persuaded...' Isabella agreed, her little face wolfish with anticipation.

'But what about you?' Freddie frowned. 'I can see them letting me and Isabella go out, but not a maid, Rose.'

'Not even if Miss Isabella asks? Can't you go on a beetle-hunting expedition? I could bring a net, or something...' Rose looked at them hopefully.

'A picnic! She can carry the basket, Freddie!' Isabella bounced in her chair. 'Oooh, yes, do let's! I love picnics!' She subsided slightly as they glared at her, but only very slightly. 'Why not? I ought to keep my strength up, if I'm going to be kidnapped. I bet Miss Sparrow only feeds her prisoners bread and water, or something horrid, like semolina. She would.'

'You will have to put me in the basket,' Gus said in a long-suffering tone. 'You can explain Rose away, but not me. Make sure there are fishpaste sandwiches, Rose.'

'And some that *aren't* fishpaste, so there's something left when we get to the park,' Isabella snapped.

'It's beneath my dignity to be sitting in a bush,' Gus complained. 'And this bush is damp.'

'Shhhhh…' Freddie and Rose hissed together.

'Oh, do hush yourselves,' Isabella whispered over her shoulder. 'Do you want everyone to hear you?'

'Are you lost, dear?' A tiny, elderly lady had paused in front of the bench where they had set their trap. Isabella was sitting alone and disconsolate, and altogether most realistic. She had assured them that she could cry on demand.

They had not considered that, of course, other people might quite innocently enquire after Isabella. They all stared suspiciously through the leaves at the old lady, but she didn't seem to be a kidnapper under a glamour.

'Oh, I am quite all right, thank you,' Isabella said firmly.

'But it's getting dark, dear. Surely you aren't here alone? You must have your mama with you, or your governess…' The old lady looked around, as if hoping that Isabella's mother would pop out of the bushes.

Isabella looked over her shoulder at Rose and Freddie, peering through the twigs, and shrugged helplessly. 'What do I do?' she whispered, as the old lady tried to signal a passing policeman with her parasol.

'For goodness' sake,' Gus muttered, and Rose felt his solid little body grow suddenly larger, and the soft white fur that she had been stroking for comfort became coarser. Then a large – very large – black wolfhound strolled out of the bushes, and took up a position in front of Isabella.

Her elderly protector turned back and gasped in fright, finding a remarkably huge set of bright white teeth just on a level with her nose.

'I'm just exercising my dog,' Isabella explained. 'I think he had gone to look for rabbits in those bushes. He is a great hunter, you see, but sadly disobedient sometimes.' Gus let at least eight inches of pink foamy tongue dangle out between his jaws, and sniffed at the parasol. 'He simply will *not* be called off, once he gives chase!' Isabella sighed, shaking her head.

The old lady backed away slowly, and then picked up her skirts and ran, not even looking back.

Isabella giggled delightedly. 'Oh, Gus, you clever old cat! That was the funniest thing I've ever seen.

Particularly as she is that interfering old tabby from across the square who told Papa he ought to send me to a ladies' seminary.'

Rose felt a frightened clutch at her shoulder, and Freddie cursed in a whisper. 'Gus, hide, it's her, it's her!'

He was right. Sweeping along the path, a black, lace-edged skirt trailing the ground, was a tall young woman. Her black clothes did not fully explain the sensation of darkness that fell over Rose as she watched Miss Sparrow approach. Maisie's locket seemed to be glowing in her hand, and she clutched it tightly, panicked in case it should somehow scream her hiding place to the kidnapper.

Gus became a very small black cat in seconds, and streaked back into the bushes. Isabella's shoulders shuddered with fear – Rose could see through the metalwork of the bench – but she dug out a lace-edged handkerchief from her reticule, and buried her face in it dolefully.

'Dear child…' Miss Sparrow had halted opposite Isabella's bench, and now bent closer to inspect her. 'May I be of assistance? Are you perhaps lost?'

Her voice was honey-sweet, and it sent sticky ripples down Rose's spine. She could *hear* the glamours in it, clanging like badly tuned bells.

'I – I don't know…' Isabella sobbed. 'My nursemaid

stopped to talk with one of the guardsmen outside the barracks, and I ran on because she took so long, and she'd promised we should go to the park. But I don't think it was *this* park, and I know I live close by, but I cannot think where!'

It was word-for-word the story they had agreed, and Rose and Freddie exchanged relieved glances. Isabella hadn't decided to embroider the lies, as they'd feared she would.

'You poor little dear,' Miss Sparrow cooed. 'Don't worry, I'm sure we shall find her. Why don't you come with me, and we'll go and look? Or do you know your address? My carriage is waiting only on the other side of the park – I can take you home directly.'

Isabella sobbed and spluttered incoherently, and Miss Sparrow seemed to tire of trying to placate her. She put a hand gently on the back of Isabella's neck, and twitched away her handkerchief. 'Why, your handkerchief is wet right through, dear child. You must borrow mine. I have a nice clean one, just here.' And she drew a handkerchief swiftly from her sleeve, and held it against Isabella's face.

Rose had one glimpse of Isabella's blue eyes glancing back towards their hiding place in sudden panic, then her eyelids drooped, and she slumped back against the sorceress's supporting arm.

SIXTEEN

The cellar was dark – a thick, black darkness that they could almost touch. Nothing like the darkness outdoors, where even in smog-ridden London, there were occasional glimpses of stars.

It smelled, too. Fifteen children using one bucket starts to smell very quickly. Rose had gagged as Miss Sparrow thrust them into the stinking darkness.

'Why didn't you rescue me?' Isabella complained. 'You didn't keep to the plan.'

'Bella, the plan didn't include her spotting us and dragging us out of the bushes!' Freddie said crossly. 'At least she didn't catch Gus. Hopefully he'll make it back to the house.'

Rose wasn't really listening to them bickering. She

217

was peering through the darkness, trying to work out where the other children were, and how many of them were imprisoned here. She could hear them breathing, very quietly, nervously.

'Who's there?' she whispered. 'Maisie, is that you? Lily?'

The silence was broken by a tiny gasp, and someone shuffled closer. 'Rose?' Maisie's voice was quavery, and she sounded disbelieving and horrified. 'Oh, Rose, she got you too! I thought you'd be safe in that grand house.'

'It's Rose! Sarah-Jane, Rose is here! Ellen, did you hear?' Lily's voice sounded as though she were bouncing up and down. 'Annie, my friend Rose!'

'We came to rescue you,' Rose admitted in a small voice. She felt rather silly. She had been imagining a dramatic rescue scene, with spells shooting all over the place, and Miss Sparrow vanquished. Instead, they had been captured themselves, and now they were dependent on the whim of a clever but unreliable cat. And if Gus did decide to help, instead of throwing in his lot with Miss Sparrow, whose magic was far more to his liking than Mr Fountain's at the moment, what could he do?

'I went back to visit everyone, you see,' Rose explained sadly. 'And you weren't there. Miss Lockwood told me an amazing story about you really being

Alberta, but you'd left your locket behind. It just didn't fit, somehow…'

'I believed her, Rose,' Maisie said, her words barely above a whisper. 'She said she was my mother. She was so pleased to see me. And then when I told her about the boat and the fountain, she knew it all, Rose!'

'It was a trick. I left you open for her, Maisie, making that stupid story up. I'm so sorry. And now we haven't even managed to get you out!'

'Don't worry, Rose,' Ellen said sadly. 'You hadn't told us stories, and it didn't make any difference. We believed anyway.'

Rose reached for Maisie's hand in the darkness. It was thinner and bonier than ever. 'Does she feed you?' she asked in a small voice. 'Us', she should have said, she supposed.

'She has to,' another voice broke in. A gruff little voice, a boy. 'She needs us strong.'

'What for?' Rose squeaked nervously.

There was a pause, as though no one really wanted to tell her. Then a faint whisper came out of the dark, from over in the corner. Rose's eyes had adjusted to the darkness a little now, and she could almost make out that the speaker was slumped on a pile of rags. Her skin glowed pale in the darkness, as though she were milk-white.

219

'Blood,' she breathed, and the word seemed to echo round the cellar. 'She takes our blood.'

Isabella made a doubtful, disgusted noise. 'What on earth *for*?'

'Amy's right. It's some horrible spell,' Maisie whispered. Rose could feel her shudder through their clasped hands. 'I saw it when she brought me here. Once she'd got me inside the door – oh, she changed, Rose, so quickly. It was like she was a different person! She even looked different, can you believe that?'

Rose felt the movement in the darkness as she and Freddie and Isabella exchanged glances. 'Oh yes,' she muttered ruefully.

'Before, when she was pretending to be my mother, she was fatter, I'm sure she was. And she talked different, softer somehow. She held me, Rose, and that's when I really believed her. I didn't think anyone could hold me like that, and say what she said, and it not be true!' Maisie's hand was burning on Rose's now, in the feverish telling of her story.

'She's a genius at glamours,' Freddie sighed. 'And a damn good liar, as well.'

Maisie was silent, and Rose realised that she had no idea who had spoken. She patted Maisie's wrist reassuringly. 'That's Freddie, Maisie, he's my master's apprentice. Mr Fountain, he's a magician, and he's enamoured of this Miss Sparrow. Well and truly gone. He wants to marry her.'

There was a hissing rush of laughter and whispers.

'Good luck to him,' Maisie said wryly. 'She'll eat him alive!'

'She shan't! She won't! I shan't let her have him!' Rose could almost swear Isabella was spitting sparks. She let go of Maisie, and grabbed Isabella before she flung herself down in a fury. Who knew what she might land on?

'And this is my mistress... Miss Bella, stop it! What's the point of squealing like that?'

'Shut her up, she'll bring the witch down on us!' the boy's voice spoke out anxiously.

Freddie and Isabella drew in their breath sharply, and Rose realised that it was a word she'd never heard used in the Fountain house. It was always 'alchemist' or 'magician'. Witch, obviously, was not a polite term. It seemed sadly amusing that they should care, just now. But at least it had shocked Isabella out of her temper.

'You won't be alive to care about him soon,' Amy's whisper came from across the room again, a faint thread, embodied a little by grim amusement.

'Amy's been here the longest,' Maisie whispered to them. 'She's been taken upstairs four times. She says she doesn't think she'll last much longer.'

'So what happened, when she brought you back to this house?' Rose asked, with horrified fascination. They had not seen much of Miss Sparrow's residence, as it had been dark when she'd bundled them out of the carriage, and she'd dragged them along the hallways and straight into the cellar.

Maisie shivered, remembering. 'When the front door banged shut, Rose, I was so happy – she'd said my father would be at home, waiting to meet me. She shut that door, and I looked around for him. I turned to ask her where he would be, and her face! It was like a monster. So white, and her eyes shining hard, like, like coal. She dragged me into a room, all full of jars, and bottles, and spirit lamps. And she picked up a knife, Rose. She'd gone so strange, I thought she was mad and she was going to kill me. But she just nicked my wrist and let the blood run out into a bowl.'

'She'd run out. We were all too worn down, and she needed more. She needed fresh blood.' Amy's giggle sounded ghostly in the dark. She wasn't much more than a ghost now.

'When I woke up I was here in the dark, with my wrist bandaged up,' Maisie explained. 'I think I fainted. I could hardly move. It was as if she'd taken all the life out of me with the blood.'

'What does she do with it?' Rose could hardly form

the words. She didn't want to hear, but she had to.

'I think – I think she drinks it,' Maisie said quietly.

'Urgh!' Isabella nestled closer to Rose. 'She wouldn't! That's cannibalism, it's horrible.'

Freddie suddenly made a little, satisfied noise, and held his hand out towards Rose and the others. He had a large glass marble sitting in his hand, one of the expensive kind, with a beautiful red and yellow flame-like spiral running through it. Now it was glowing softly, and making his hand glow too, so that his fingers had red cracks in them. Rose had never realised just how comforting light was until she'd missed it. Everyone in the cellar sighed, and crawled towards it, so that they were sitting in a close, huddled group, gazing at the tiny light.

'A magician's apprentice,' Amy breathed. 'I didn't believe you before.' The light made her skin look as thin as paper.

'Can't do much yet,' Freddie said shyly. 'But I'm quite good at lights and flames. That sort of thing. Just took me a while to think of what to put it in.'

Rose looked round anxiously, now that she could see what was what. There were fifteen others as well as themselves. Lily seemed to be the youngest, and Amy looked like the oldest, but perhaps just because she was so worn out from the blood-letting.

Lily was sitting cuddled up against another little girl about her own age, who Rose decided had to be Annie, the girl the street children had lost. They both had their thumbs in their mouths, and they were leaning on a girl in the ruin of an expensive nightgown. She had to be the one from the newspaper, who'd been snatched from her bed.

'Magic,' the gruff-voiced boy muttered, staring distrustfully but hungrily at the light.

He was wearing livery a little like Bill's, Rose realised. She was willing to bet that he was Bill's friend, Jack. He hadn't run off to join the circus after all, she thought sadly. 'Not all magic's bad,' she protested.

'Rose can do it!' Maisie boasted. 'She makes pictures.'

'She worked out who'd taken you as well.' Freddie glanced up from the light at Maisie. 'She looked for you in a mirror. It was really clever magic.'

'Oh, Rose,' Maisie said gratefully.

Rose shook her head dismissively. 'I still don't understand what it is she's doing. I wish Gus were here, Freddie. Can you think of anything? Anything from those letters she sent to Mr Fountain?'

Freddie frowned at the marble light, trying to remember.

Suddenly there was a clicking noise as the hammers of a heavy lock fell into place, and the door swung open. Miss Sparrow stood in the doorway, holding up a candle. It made her look monstrous, a huge shadow falling away behind her, and the light glittering horribly in her black eyes.

Luckily, Freddie had thrust the marble into his pocket as soon as he'd heard the noise, and it seemed Miss Sparrow hadn't noticed it. She walked into the cellar and held up the lantern, examining the children. Then she stooped down, like a hawk hunting her prey, and seized Amy by the arm, jerking her to her feet. Amy hung limply from her grasp, like a rag doll, not even complaining.

The others complained for her.

'Not Amy again!' Sarah-Jane gasped. 'You can't! You'll kill her! Can't you see she's half-dead already, you mean old witch!'

Freddie scrambled up and tried to lift Amy back to her feet, but Miss Sparrow batted him away with a sweep of her hand, and he fell to the floor, gasping. A trickle of blood ran down from his nose, and Miss Sparrow watched it eagerly. Rose shuddered as a pale, pointed tongue licked out over her lips.

'Don't waste it, don't waste it,' Miss Sparrow mumbled, seemingly to herself, almost unaware of the children listening, as Rose passed Freddie a handkerchief. 'Little mage-children's blood... Three of them, all at once.

Stronger blood. Maybe that's what it needs. Later, we'll try… After this one… This one could be the key, anyway…' Then she shook herself slightly and tore her gaze away from the red-stained linen. 'Your turn later,' she said, smiling round at Rose and Isabella and Freddie. She licked her lips again, and her eyes lingered on Rose's handkerchief. Then she dragged Amy out, and the door slammed once more. Freddie drew the marble out of his pocket cautiously.

'I can't believe she took Amy again,' the girl in the nightgown said, shaking her head slowly. 'Why? It isn't as if she can have much blood left! She's so weak she hardly stand up.'

'Alice is right. It'll be the death of her.' Maisie stared miserably at the floor.

The others nodded. 'Why didn't she just use one of us?' Jack asked angrily. 'We wouldn't go and die and mess up her nice laboratory!'

Rose gulped, and gave a strange, retching little moan. She'd just had a truly horrible thought – and she realised too late that she probably ought to have kept it to herself.

'What?' Freddie demanded, his hand still gingerly cupping his bleeding nose.

Rose looked round at them all unhappily, and whispered, 'Maybe she *wants* her to die.'

SEVENTEEN

Rose stared at the dirty floor of the cellar, not wanting to meet anyone's eyes. She almost felt ashamed for even thinking such a horrible thing, let alone saying it.

'Why on earth would she *want* Amy to die?' Freddie asked blankly.

Rose looked apologetically at them all. 'She said that maybe Amy was the key, as though there was something different about her, something special. But the only different thing is that – well, that she's dying... So perhaps she wants her to. She drinks the blood, doesn't she?' She looked questioningly at the others, and they nodded doubtfully. 'And it's for a spell? Maybe she thinks that dying blood is different, *better*. The last drop of Amy's lifeblood...' And here her voice faltered to a whisper, as though it were too awful to speak aloud.

'That's horrible.' Isabella hissed disgustedly.

'I think she's right, though.' Jack nodded, frowning as he tried to remember. 'She said something once, when she was taking my blood, about *new life*. I think she thought I was unconscious – or maybe she just didn't care if I heard, I don't know. She was watching the blood dripping into her silver bowl, and it was like she was counting every drop. That's when she said it.'

'I reckon you're onto something there, Jack,' Maisie nodded, and the others looked as though, unwillingly, they also agreed.

'And if Amy loses her life with the blood, Miss Sparrow thinks the life-spark will come into the blood she's stolen.' Freddie shook his head slowly. 'You're right. She *is* a witch.'

'So...is she trying to live for ever?' Rose asked, feeling confused.

'And that's why she's catching children!' Jack exclaimed. 'It isn't just that they're easier to seize, they've got more life left!'

'Eternal life,' Freddie said wonderingly. 'It's the other great mystery. Alchemists have been searching for centuries,' he explained. 'How to turn base metals –

that's lead and stuff – into gold, they've solved that one – that's what our master does – and the other one is the secret of eternal life. No one's managed that yet. Or at least, they haven't lived to tell the tale.' He sniggered, then remembered where he was, and wiped the grin off his face. 'Sorry. I mean, it's the big question now. It's only a matter of time before someone solves it. That must have been why she was writing to Mr Fountain. She thought that because he was one of the alchemists who discovered the gold solution, he might be able to help her with everlasting life, too.'

'Your master can make gold?' Maisie asked Rose, her eyes like saucers.

Rose shrugged. 'Apparently. I've never seen him do it, mind.'

'Oh, he can,' Freddie assured them. 'It's actually not that difficult.' He frowned. 'Of course, that's why he was doubtful about her. She must have let slip some of her ideas in her letters to him. Fountain may be an old bear to his apprentices, but he'd never stomach drinking blood.'

'That's my father you're talking about,' Isabella muttered. 'But I suppose he is a bit of a bear sometimes. Anyway, whatever she's trying to do, it doesn't really matter now. We have to stop her! We need to make a plan. She's coming back, and she's going to do it to us next!' She held out her pretty little hands, gazing at her wrists in fascinated horror.

Everyone else in the cellar stared at her, and Isabella shuffled closer to Rose. 'I don't mean it like that. Really! What I'm saying is, is…that if it's all three of us together, surely we have more chance of fighting back! There!' She looked round in relief. 'We should make use of the opportunity, don't you see?'

Jack glared at her distrustfully. 'Perhaps. But just remember she's had blood from all the rest of us at least once, little witch-girl. It's your turn next. Why should you escape, eh?' He held his bandaged wrist under her nose threateningly and Isabella recoiled. There was dried blood spotting it, and it smelled bad.

'I know!' she gasped.

Freddie put his arm round her. 'Leave her alone,' he told Jack, his voice rather high and nervous. Jack was somewhat bigger than he was. 'She's only little. She didn't mean it like that.'

Jack scowled. 'She's a spoilt little princess,' he muttered, but he seemed impressed that Freddie had stood up to him.

'Not arguing with you on that one.' Freddie gave a gracious nod. Then he sighed, and held up the marble. 'If this is what we've got to fight with, I don't think much of our chances.'

'Can't you do anything, well, *better*?' the girl in the nightgown – Alice, the others had called her – asked him in an apologetic tone. 'I don't mean to be rude,' she added hastily.

'I do,' Jack put in. 'Can't you throw balls of fire or something? You're right, mate, a shiny marble's getting us nowhere.'

'None of us are trained magicians, you see,' Freddie explained wretchedly. 'We all three have power, but we can't control it properly yet. We're just no match for her.'

Rose shook her head. 'There must be some way to make us stronger,' she said. She'd been searching through the pocket of her cloak, looking for anything that might possibly be used as a weapon, but all she'd found was Maisie's locket. She looped the chain around her fingers, twisting and pulling at it as she thought.

'Oh! Rose, is that my locket?' Maisie jumped up and then kneeled hopefully in front of Rose. 'Oh, it is, it is! You brought it back from St Bridget's for me!'

Rose smiled distractedly at her. 'I'm sorry, Maisie, I'd forgotten. Take it, here.' She hadn't really been concentrating on Maisie, but as the tarnished chain slipped into her friend's fingers, Maisie's face caught her attention. Her eyes were bright with tears, but she looked so happy. She seemed stronger, her face losing its sad, waif-like look. Her cheeks almost filled out, though that was surely impossible. Maisie suddenly looked twice as alive as she had the minute before. All because of a tawdry little trinket.

Rose looked at it. It wasn't magical. She knew it wasn't. It was a rubbishy old locket, made of tin.

Maisie held it up. 'Ever since that devil said she was my…*mother*…I've been wishing and wishing for this back. This was my real mother's. I know I'll never see her, Rose, don't worry, I'm cured of that. But I still want this to help me think of her, that's all.'

The locket seemed to glow as it dangled from her fingers, but Rose was almost sure that was only the way they were all staring at it. Maisie's love for it made it special, that was all.

But perhaps that was all they needed?

Look at what the locket had done for Maisie. She was ready to take on a hundred witches now. If only they all had something so special. Rose sighed. They didn't, of course. She had no locket, not even a lock of her mother's hair. Nothing to make her feel strong at all.

Rose stared unseeingly at the rough bricks of the wall. Did it actually need to be a *thing*? Couldn't a thought do as well? She'd lasted all these years at the orphanage with just one thought – that one day she would get out, have a job, and earn a wage, and order her life her own way. It had kept her going. Didn't that make it her locket? Her talisman? It was even more special now, that treasured plan, because she'd managed it at last, and now some madwoman was trying to take it away from her.

'What is it?' Freddie asked her quietly.

Rose looked at him, her eyes hopeful. 'I think I've had an idea, something that we can do.' She turned back to the others. 'Does anyone else have a precious thing, like Maisie's locket? Maybe not here with you, but something special? Something that makes you feel happy and safe?'

Alice nodded sadly. 'My pony, Frisky. He'll be missing me dreadfully.'

Jack brought out a pocket knife. 'My dad's, it was. He's gone off fighting in the war, he gave it me to look after for him. Too bad I didn't get to use it on that witch upstairs. I tried, but she's stronger than she looks...' He shivered.

Rose blinked, remembering. Bill had told her that Jack always swore his dad was coming back for him. She felt even more determined to make this work. If magic could rescue Bill's friend, perhaps he would trust her again... She didn't have time to think about it now. The others were nodding eagerly, telling each other, showing off special treasures. Annie's was only a button

233

she'd found dropped in the street, but she clearly loved it.

'I knew it!' Rose's heart thudded with sudden excitement. She held Freddie's arm. 'Can't we use that somehow? If we all think of the special things, can't we tie that power together? Have you got anything?'

Freddie nodded slowly and held out the marble. 'I know it isn't much, but I thought up how to do it by myself, and at just the right time, too. I'm proud of it,' he whispered, a little embarrassed. Then his eyes widened. 'Rose! I've already put the light in it, and we've all been using the light, depending on it. So we're bound to the light already. I don't think it would be too difficult to put our strength from the treasures into it, too.'

'How?' Maisie asked simply, staring at the little glowing light.

Freddie looked round at them helplessly. 'A tying spell? I know one for parcels…'

'Hold hands, for a start,' Isabella spoke up. She'd been remarkably silent until now, cowed by Jack. 'And then think of your special things inside the light, I suppose. Freddie had better hold it, and say the spell.'

Everyone scrabbled to find their neighbour's hand. Rose found herself holding Maisie's on one side, and covering Freddie's hand on the marble with her other hand. The light seemed to pulse in time with their heartbeats. 'Now think!' she begged them all.

All at once a great surge of strength and calm flowed through her and over her and round her. Images of a small black horse eating sugar from her hand, dreams of falling asleep with a real mother stroking her hair, pure happiness at finding a sparkling treasure in the mud – they filled her mind. It seemed hours until they faded away, leaving her so calm, so certain. Rose blinked, and shivered delightedly, and looked round at the others. They had seen the memories too, she could tell. She had never seen Freddie look so at peace with himself. It made her see how before he had always been frightened, or angry, or doubting.

'So what are we going to do?' Isabella demanded, wriggling with excitement. 'How are we going to rescue Amy?'

'And what are we going to do with that witch when we've done it?' Jack asked in grim voice. 'We'll have to kill her, I reckon.'

Some of Rose's precious happiness ebbed away a little. 'Can't we just grab Amy and knock Sparrow out, maybe?' she said faintly.

'So she can do this to more kids when she wakes up?' jeered Jack.

It was horribly true. 'The police?' Rose suggested.

Freddie shook his head doubtfully. 'I don't think they'd take our word for it, not children. Besides, she'd use a glamour, wouldn't she? She'd have them eating out of her hand in no time. Look what she did to Isabella's father – and he understands glamours. The poor policeman would have no chance.' He frowned. 'But if we could get Mr Fountain to see what she'd done to him, he'd be furious... *He* could tell the police, and stop her enchanting them. If we knocked her out and brought him back here to bind her, that would work, I think.'

Jack was still in favour of killing her, but the rest were with Freddie.

'Doesn't make any difference if we can't get out of here and go for her anyway,' Jack said sulkily, and the others were forced to agree. No one had quite thought of the solid, heavy, *locked* door until now. It didn't even shake when they tried to pound on it with their fists, and Isabella hurt her foot kicking it.

Rose sat down on the stone step in front of the door, her nails sore from scrabbling at the lock. 'We'll have to wait until she brings back Amy, and rush her then.' It wasn't a good solution. They'd wanted to spare Amy another blood-letting, but she couldn't see what else to do.

'But – what if she doesn't bring Amy back?'

Alice said, in a quiet, sad little voice.

Everyone stared at her.

Alice blinked timidly. 'Amy said she wouldn't last another time. She was so sure. She said she could feel it. If she's – dead – then why would Miss Sparrow bring her back?'

There was silence. Then Rose stood up and hammered angrily on the silvery wood. 'You're right. We have to get this door open, and go and get Amy back before that old demon kills her.'

'Can't you magic it open?' Maisie asked Rose and Freddie hopefully.

'Rose, can you make old wood move? Like you did with that wisteria before?' Freddie suggested.

Rose laid a doubtful hand against the weathered wood of the door. It was smooth and cold and so dead. It didn't speak to her like the creeper had. Here was no life to plead with. 'No,' she sighed.

'I don't want to waste this,' Freddie said, looking down at the marble. It was glowing so brightly in his hand now, it seemed to burn with an eagerness to be used. 'But I suppose if we can't even get out…'

'Annie could open the door!' It was Lily, piping up from behind all the older children. The two littlest ones had been sitting watching, thumbs in mouths, but now Lily was on tiptoe, jigging from foot to foot excitedly.

'Don't be silly,' Sarah-Jane said scornfully, and Ellen and Maisie looked as though they agreed with her. But Lily hauled Annie up, and dragged the ragged little girl through to the door. 'Look!' she said simply, and Annie took her thumb out of her mouth too, and pulled a set of wire lockpicks from the pocket of her filthy little apron.

EIGHTEEN

Annie had the door open in the space of two minutes, as the others looked on in amazement.

'Where did you learn to do that?' Rose asked admiringly.

'I should think her thieving brothers taught her,' Freddie muttered. 'She's the one we promised to look for, isn't she, Rose? She probably carries the lockpicks in case they're stopped by a constable.' He still had a grudge against the boys for attacking them. 'Anyway, thank goodness it isn't bolted on the other side, else we'd have been well and truly scuppered.'

But the door swung open easily, revealing a gloomy flight of steps up, and the occupants of the cellar crept cautiously out.

The steps led into the kitchen, which was deserted and unlit, and very different from the warm, welcoming room at the Fountain house.

'Doesn't she have any servants?' Rose murmured in surprise.

'I suppose she can't risk them finding out what she's doing,' Freddie mused. 'Perhaps the house has a spell on it to keep it clean, though I've never heard of one.' He peeped out of the kitchen door and up another staircase. 'This leads to the hallway, doesn't it? I don't remember much from when she brought us down here.'

Rose blinked. She didn't remember anything. She'd been terrified, and had spent most of the carriage journey with her eyes closed, hoping she wasn't going to be sick.

The hallway was patterned with black and white tiles, and looked very pretty, just like a normal sort of house. There was an elephant's foot umbrella holder, and an occasional table with a fern in a big blue and white pot. No blood. No sign of Amy. One of the doors off the hallway was ajar, and a bar of light showed down the side of it.

'That's her workroom,' Alice whispered. She had gone pale at the sight of it, and her eyes were all black pupil, no blue left at all. Lily and Annie were pressed close against her, thumbs firmly in mouths again.

Rose felt guilty – the workroom didn't make her feel more frightened than the rest of the house, but then, she'd never been in it. Almost all the others were shielding their wrists without realising it.

'I think the little ones should go,' she whispered.

The older children looked longingly towards the door, but nodded.

'Alice had better take them, the two littlest ones, and Isabella, and you four...' Jack sorted out the younger children, and pushed them gently down the hallway.

'But I should come with you,' Alice protested guiltily, though her voice had gone high with relief.

'Just get them out of here,' Sarah-Jane urged. 'Lily, behave, or else!'

Lily nodded emphatically round her thumb.

'You'll have to be silent going past that door,' Freddie reminded them.

The older children watched as the little group pattered down the hall and waited anxiously by the door, as Alice fought with the lock. The key was in it, but it screeched, and everyone waited for the workroom door to fly open and Miss Sparrow to run screaming out. But at last it opened, and the children slipped quietly round it, Alice sending the others one last hopeful, grateful smile as she drew it closed behind her.

Rose let out a tiny sigh. It would have been so easy for them all to follow her. But they'd rescued them – that was what they'd come to do, after all. She should be glad. She exchanged a relieved half-smile with Freddie, and was about to ask what anyone thought they should do next, when Jack muttered, 'A cat!'

Padding over the black-and-white tiles was a portly white cat, with one orange eye and one blue. He rubbed his head affectionately against Rose's skirts, and she bent to lift him up. 'Gus! Did you follow us?'

'Of course,' grumbled the cat. 'I came in when Isabella and all those other children went out. How long has that madwoman been collecting children for? I'd been waiting outside for ages, no windows open, not a crack I could find anywhere. I was just about to give up and go home to fetch Fountain when I saw the door open.'

Maisie put her hand on Rose's arm. 'He talks!' she whispered delightedly. 'You've got a magic cat, Rose!' For a moment she seemed to have forgotten her fear, and Rose realised that Gus probably had some extremely strong spell on him – a charm for charm, that made almost everyone happy to see him. It was probably why he was so fat.

Gus looked at Maisie with his head on one side. 'She can hear me. Is she another magician?' His voice was doubtful; clearly he didn't think Maisie looked very magical.

Rose shook her head. 'Freddie did a spell, binding all our power. So maybe all of us have a bit of magic now.'

'Can we stroke him?' Ellen asked, her eyes wide with admiration.

'Ask *me*, if you don't mind,' Gus said haughtily. 'She doesn't own me. And yes, you may, if you have clean hands.' He closed his eyes happily as the children stroked him. It seemed a silly thing to be doing just then, but Rose could see the sparks of magic rising off Gus's silky coat, filling the admiring children with hope. Hope worked. They needed it right now, as they had very little else.

'Is there a plan?' Gus asked, butting Rose's chin.

'Only that she's in there, we think.' Freddie pointed to the workroom. 'And she's got Amy, one of the girls. We have to get Amy out, Gus, we think Miss Sparrow wants to kill her. She's trying to find a way to live for ever, you know.'

'Ridiculous. I knew she was mad,' Gus said gloomily. 'I wish old Fountain had never got mixed up with her. The worst of it is, madness works so terribly well with magic. Oh well. I can go and spy round the door for you, if you like. I'll be able to sense any guard spells with my whiskers.' He jumped down lightly from

Rose's arms, and stalked down the hallway, carefully inserting his whiskers into the gap in the door. The others followed cautiously, until they were gathered in a kind of ring, watching the cat edging into the room.

He seemed to be gone for ever, but it was perhaps only a minute until he was back, creeping out of the door with ears laid back and his whiskers drooping like an ancient Mandarin's moustache.

'What is it?' Rose asked anxiously.

'I think the girl on the couch is dead,' Gus admitted reluctantly, and there was a low moan of disbelief. They had done so well escaping from their prison – to be denied Amy was unbearable.

'If only we'd been faster,' Maisie whispered, and Rose put an arm around her.

'What's the witch doing?' Jack demanded, and Gus blinked at him. 'That's the strange thing. She seems half-dead too. Or fainting at least. She's slumped on the floor by the couch.'

'Let's get her!' Jack snarled, springing forwards to the door, but Freddie grabbed him back.

'Slowly!' he hissed. 'She's a – a witch, remember? Don't go dashing in like that.' He peered carefully round the door, Jack with him, and Rose and Maisie followed.

Gus was right. Miss Sparrow lay against the couch, quite still, a trickle of blood running from the corner of her mouth. But it was Amy who drew their eyes. She was half-falling from the cushions, one arm trailing along the floor. If they had thought she was pale before, now her skin had a deadly greenish tinge. The slit in her wrist was not even bleeding; it gaped sluggishly open.

'Let's get her out of here.' Jack's voice caught miserably, and the others came forward to help him.

Amy's black hair fell over their hands as they tried to lift her, and Rose couldn't help stroking it. It felt alive, even if Amy didn't. It was soft and sleek. How could Amy be dead and still have such pretty hair?

'Freddie,' Rose murmured. 'Give her the marble.'

'Rose, she's—'

'So it won't make any difference, will it? Just try.'

Freddie kneeled in front of the couch, and wrapped Amy's hands around the marble. The wound in her wrist flexed horribly as he touched her fingers, and he gagged. But the light flushed Amy's icy fingers pink, and they twitched.

'It's working!' Maisie whispered. 'Quick, let's hurry!' Maisie, Ellen, Sarah-Jane and Jack grabbed Amy and hauled her out of the room into the hallway, Gus running before them with his tail raised like a flag.

Rose stayed behind. If she went out into the street she didn't think she would have the courage to come back. Not when she could run. So it was better not to go, because Miss Sparrow wasn't dead. Rose could see her breathing. She knew it was stupid to stay – foolhardy. But she'd stopped that mist-monster without knowing what she'd done. Maybe the same luck would save her now.

Miss Sparrow opened her eyes. They were like beads, Rose thought, small and not very pretty. Or more like boot-buttons, actually, round and dull. The alchemist wasn't beautiful at all. Then she seemed to wake up a little more, and she shook out her hair, which was coming loose from its pins. All at once her eyes were deep and dark again, and her face exquisitely painted. She had control of her glamours now. She seized something that was lying in the folds of her black silk dress, and sprang up, towering over Rose. She was tall anyway, but the glamours had an edge of fear-magic to them, and she seemed a giantess.

What she was holding was a knife.

A silver knife, Rose noted with a sort of panicky attention to detail, as it came closer. She'd already spent considerable time polishing silver at the Fountain house, and she knew a hallmark when she saw one. A very shiny, very sharp, silver knife.

'Rose!'

Rose jumped, luckily backwards. The knife had

mesmerised her, and in a couple more steps Miss Sparrow would have had it at her throat.

Freddie seized her tightly as she stumbled, and hissed, 'What were you *doing*?'

'Later,' Gus mewed.

'There is no later…' Miss Sparrow told them gently, the knife weaving in front of them. 'Two mage-children's blood will have to do. The other girl was useless after all, I was wrong, I admit. Silver, and the lifeblood, I was so sure…'

'She's mad,' Rose muttered.

'Being mad doesn't make her knife any less sharp.' Gus's claws scratched on the parquet floor as they edged backwards, and Miss Sparrow seemed to realise that her prey was perilously close to the door. Her face at once became ten times more beautiful, so perfect that it was terrifyingly wrong, like one of Isabella's expensive dolls come to life.

They couldn't defeat anything so lovely, Rose knew. If they fought, they might spoil her. They should stop. Stand still. Give in.

But what about the blood? Rose asked herself suddenly. *A minute ago she had blood dripping down her chin, and now it's gone. Just like Gus eating too much to be a thin cat.*

So this isn't real!

Rose's eyes snapped open, and she poked Freddie in the side, hard. 'Wake up! She glamoured us again!' She picked Gus up, and shook him a little.

'Fish!' he mewed sharply, and then shuddered and stared at Miss Sparrow. 'The cheek of it! Glamouring a cat.'

Miss Sparrow had taken a step back, and was wiping the blood from her face with a delicate lace handkerchief, eyeing them cautiously. Clearly they were more of a threat than she had suspected, and the strong spell had tired her.

Unfortunately, even tired, she was more than a match for two untrained children, even though they had Gus to help them. Rose suspected that Gus was actually a lot more powerful than he let everyone think. But Miss Sparrow had still caught him with a glamour – and it had been Rose who broke them out of it.

Gus put his paws on Rose's shoulder, and purred encouragingly in her ear. *Rose, you are the strongest of us against her. The glamours don't work well on you. She will try again, harder, any moment. Freddie, whatever happens, believe Rose!*

Rose nodded, gulping nervously, and Freddie scowled but reluctantly murmured, 'Yes, I know…' He moved to stand slightly behind her, as though he was admitting she was the stronger one.

Believe Rose…

Rose held Gus tightly, staring at Miss Sparrow, waiting for her to strike.

'She's not doing anything! Why isn't she doing anything?' she whispered to Gus.

'Be on your guard,' Gus hissed back. 'She's tricky.'

Miss Sparrow seemed to have decided that Rose was her main enemy too. She walked forwards, very slowly, with her hands stretched out, and a lovely smile on her face. Only the chalk whiteness of her skin spoilt it.

Rose took a step back, and then another, her hands tightening in Gus's fur.

We've made a mistake, she howled in her head. *She isn't going to glamour us, she's just going to kill us! Help!*

She can't, Gus said, a little doubtfully. *All her power is in her glamours. She won't be able to strike us with anything real. At least…I don't think so…*

Are you sure? Rose begged, as she backed up against Freddie, and Freddie backed up against the door. *I think she could kill us pretty easily. It feels like she only needs to touch us. And she's still got the knife!*

And Freddie reminded him, *You said believe Rose! Now what do I do?*

'Little Rose,' Miss Sparrow murmured as she came closer still, the point of the knife trembling. 'A new

249

witch.' She smiled wider. 'Oh, yes, I use the old words. You're a witch, just like me. You could be so powerful. So special. So rich. No more slaving, Rose. Come with me, and I'll teach you. You could do so much!'

Rose blinked at her. Miss Sparrow was strong. Determined. *Just like me*, Rose couldn't help thinking. The temptation was very great. Never having to sweep up someone else's mess again...

'Why are you wearing that dowdy cotton dress, Rose darling? You should be dressed in velvet, lace, fur...'

Rose's clouded eyes suddenly cleared. It was only another kind of glamour. Possibly it was the truth, too, but that didn't make it *right*. She'd made this dress. There was a spot of blood on the hemline where she'd jabbed the sewing needle into her finger. She'd had to hide it from Miss Bridges.

Blood. She'd forgotten. How could she have considered, even for a minute, throwing in her lot with someone who'd stolen children's blood and drunk it? Rose shuddered.

Miss Sparrow saw. 'Stupid child!' she snarled. 'So arrogant, so *good*! See how far it gets you now!' Her voice rose to a scream, and she dropped the knife and flung herself at Rose, her fingernails lengthening to horny claws as she made to tear out Rose's throat.

'Rose, is this just a glamour, because she looks like

she's going to kill you and I don't know what to do!' Freddie yelled.

'No!' Rose yelled. 'It's real, help me get her – oh!' She gulped with relief as Freddie hit Miss Sparrow with an umbrella stand. The witch reeled away, gasping, and spitting blood again.

'Thanks!' Rose gasped.

'Don't mention it,' Freddie muttered grimly, watching Miss Sparrow wiping the blood away from her eyes. 'I nipped out into the hallway while she was trying to con you onto her side. You were both too wrapped up in each other to notice.' He flicked Rose a rather bitter little smile. 'That pays for you saving me and Gus from the spirit, anyway.'

Rose was hardly listening. Miss Sparrow still looked shaken, and she hadn't bothered to hide the blood dripping from her face, or put her hair back into its ordered curls. But she had picked up her silver knife again, and she was holding it in front of her, her hands writhing and twisting in shapes that looked awful and meaningful and dangerous.

'Do you think we could make it if we just ran?' Freddie said hopefully.

Rose looked at Miss Sparrow, and then back at Freddie. 'No.'

'Then the only thing I can think of to do is

call that elemental spirit up again.'

'What, the mist-monster?' Rose whispered.

Freddie scowled at her. 'It's not a – yes, all right, the *mist-monster.*'

Gus glared at him over Rose's shoulder. 'Do you not remember the last time? How exactly are we going to get it to do what we want?'

Freddie shrugged, still staring at Miss Sparrow, who seemed to be recovering worryingly quickly. 'Elemental spirits are attracted to life force, power – you know, all that sort of thing. I had to listen to a great long lecture about it last week. She's much more powerful than we are, you can't deny that. Anyway, it's got to go for us or her, which means we have half a chance. Which is better than none at all, isn't it? Can you remember the spell?'

'Of course I can...' Gus started to chant in a low voice, and Freddie joined him, while Rose stared at Miss Sparrow. Her hair seemed to be growing back into its elaborate curls and coils, which Rose thought probably meant she was regaining her strength. 'Hurry up,' she urged.

Freddie scowled, but waved his left hand in a beckoning sort of gesture, and all at once that strange, malevolent buzzing filled the room.

A coil of greyish smoke was rising through the cracks in the parquet, making them ripple. More and more of it came, and it had eyes, and teeth too this time. It quested towards Rose, then drew back cautiously as she hissed at it. Then its attention switched to Freddie and Gus, and it knew them. The buzzing deepened to a horribly satisfied purr, and it advanced again.

'Look for the knife,' Gus mewed, stepping back. 'See the blood! That way!' And the creature swirled and saw Miss Sparrow for the first time. She was holding out her knife, but her eyes were frightened, and Rose suddenly realised that glamours didn't work on mist, and Miss Sparrow knew that too. But so much of her power was poured into the spells which encased her, that she didn't have anything left to fight with. The creature seemed to swell as it eased towards her, intrigued. Hungry.

Miss Sparrow muttered spells and charms and incantations in a desperate litany, but the mist thickened, and darkened.

How did I get rid of something so strong? Without knowing what I was doing? The questions flickered at the back of Rose's mind. Pure luck, she supposed.

The creature covered Miss Sparrow, her spells crackling and fizzing gently as it licked them up.

'Let's go.' Rose snatched up Gus and backed towards the door. 'If it finishes her off, it might come after us for seconds.'

They dashed down the hallway and slammed the big front door behind them, shutting Miss Sparrow and the mist-monster in together.

The street was dark, and a London fog was wreathing round the gas lamps, making Rose search for hungry little eyes as they ran home, scurrying through street after street.

'Will it chase us?' she muttered in Gus's ear as they hurried through a particularly dense patch.

'No. It'll go back to sleep it off. Probably. Can we go any faster?' Gus peered ahead through the fog. 'Ah, we're coming to our square!'

The mist was thick in the square too, but as they approached the Fountain house they could see golden light shining from the drawing-room windows, and pouring down the steps from the open front door.

On the steps was a tall figure, shrugging on a coat, and impatiently waving away the mufflers and umbrellas and galoshes that were being pressed upon him by his staff. 'Do as Isabella says, Miss Bridges, feed them all whatever you can find. I shall be back soon, I dearly hope. No, not the carriage, I haven't time, I shall find a cab.' He set off down the steps, and Gus leaped from Rose's arms and streaked across the road to meet him.

'Sir! Sir! We're back!'

Freddie hastened after him, and Rose followed,

a little hesitantly.

'Frederick! You're safe.' Mr Fountain seized his hands and scanned his face anxiously. 'Not harmed, dear boy? That despicable woman! The enchantments lifted a few moments ago. Where is she?'

'They lifted when the elemental spirit got her,' Gus said smugly.

'Elemental spirit?' Mr Fountain raised his eyebrows. 'Tell me!'

Freddie and Gus spilled out the story eagerly, standing on the steps, and Mr Fountain stared at them, occasionally shaking his head in amazement.

'Incredible. Quite incredible. Go on into the house. I want you to tell me all of it properly when I return. You too, Rose, I particularly want to talk to *you*.'

'Are you going to Miss Sparrow's house?' Freddie whispered anxiously.

Mr Fountain stared out across the square, towards the way they'd come. 'I want to see what's left of her.' His voice was grim. 'Go on, inside, all of you. Go and rest. Isabella has the children in the drawing room. I will be back very soon.'

He ushered them in with great flaps of his coat, up the steps and through the great front door – even Rose. She stood shivering in the hallway, with Miss Bridges eyeing her sternly. Gus ran in to claim a place in front of the drawing-room fire, and Freddie went gratefully after him, rubbing his hands in the warmth. Rose watched them, a little sadly, then bobbed a curtsey to Miss Bridges. She couldn't go in there. She wasn't even allowed to clean in there. 'Sorry I'm late back, Miss,' she murmured.

'Oh, go on with them, silly child,' Miss Bridges sighed. 'There's half an orphanage in there as it is, and the police to be called. I shouldn't think any of us will be in bed till midnight.' She shooed Rose towards the drawing room, and sped down the hallway, calling for Susan and beef tea.

Rose grinned as she peered through the door. The elegant drawing room was covered in pillows and eiderdowns, and the children were gathered in a ring in front of the fire, with Amy swathed in blankets on the sofa right in the middle. Isabella was in her element dispensing hot chocolate, while her governess flapped pitifully at the sight of grubby urchins all over the best furniture.

'Rose!'

Rose spun round, wide-eyed, her fingernails digging into her palms – in the last few hours, that sort of hissing whisper had generally meant that something very scary was about to happen.

'It's me, don't look so worried.' It was Bill, lurking by

the green baize door and looking furtive. 'Can't be long, Miss Bridges'll cut my ears off if she finds me hanging about right now.'

'Did you see him? Your friend Jack? Was it him?' Rose asked hopefully. 'I didn't get much chance to ask him, but I reckon it must be.'

Bill nodded approvingly. 'Snatched in the street, his household can't blame him for that. Not if Miss Bridges tells them it's the truth. He'll get his place back, let's hope.' He smiled at Rose, but then leaned closer and frowned at her. 'Next time you're going off to do something stupid with Mr Freddie, let alone Miss Bella, you take me along with you! What were you thinking?'

'That you hate magic! You wouldn't even look at me properly after the treacle and the horse! You kept looking like I was something disgusting you'd got on your boots!' Rose protested.

Bill shrugged, rather shamefaced. 'Not your fault, I suppose. You're afflicted. You can't help it. And you got Jack out of that place. He said he was shut in the cellar. And someone had cut him about.' Bill patted her awkwardly on the arm. 'That was brave,' he said quietly.

'So is Freddie brave, too?' Rose enquired sweetly.

'Him! Too stupid to know what he was doing, I should think,' Bill retorted irritably. 'Get on into the drawing room, you, that white demon's looking for you.'

Gus was standing in the drawing-room doorway, staring meaningfully at Rose. She nodded to him, and he whisked back into the room. 'I'll be down to the kitchen in a minute, I should think,' she told Bill.

Bill gulped, and stepped backwards, and Rose turned to see Mr Fountain coming in, having opened his own front door, which was unheard of. Bill oiled himself out of the way so quickly it almost seemed like magic, and Rose was left looking silly by the drawing-room door.

'Shall I take your coat, Sir?' she squeaked, dropping a clumsy curtsey.

Mr Fountain looked at her consideringly. 'No. I think not.' He sounded quite out of breath, as though he'd run all the way from Miss Sparrow's house. But Rose couldn't imagine him ever running. He laid his coat over an occasional table instead, and Rose's eyes widened in dismay. Miss Bridges would be horrified. 'Come on.' He swept her into the drawing room before him, and sat down in a large armchair, slowly removing his gloves. 'There was nothing left. Nothing. Except for a large amount of equipment that I really don't want to think about.' He glanced at the children clustered round Isabella, his gaze resting for a while on Amy and her bandaged wrists, and sighed.

'Sir, we need you to listen, it's very important.' Freddie stood in front of Mr Fountain's chair, and Gus leaped on the arm, and they both talked, mostly at the same time, and mostly about Rose, while she listened, squirming.

'So you see, Sir, you have to take her on as an apprentice,' Freddie wound up earnestly.

'Really very strong magic.' Gus nodded. 'Quite talented.'

Mr Fountain looked over at Rose, waiting some way behind his chair. 'And what do you say about it?'

'Thank you, Sir, but I don't want to be an apprentice. It wouldn't be fitting.' Rose curtseyed again.

'Oh, don't start that again,' Freddie groaned. 'For heaven's sake, Sir, she can talk to trees!'

'Which is precisely why I don't want to make Rose do anything she doesn't want to do.' Mr Fountain held out his hand, and Rose came slowly across the room. She hadn't quite meant to, and she had a feeling that he was quite as good at glamours as Miss Sparrow. 'So what *do* you want to do?'

'The same as now?' Rose suggested hopefully.

'It does seem rather a waste.' Mr Fountain sounded apologetic. 'Your power is so strong. Perhaps lessons in between polishing?' He waved a hand thoughtfully, clearly unsure quite what his servants did all day. 'I could persuade Miss Bridges, I'm sure.'

Rose nodded, and curtseyed again. 'If it doesn't get in the way of my duties, Sir,' she murmured.

'I can see that you might be very useful,' Mr Fountain mused, stroking his moustache. 'So, Rose, I've had Frederick's account, and Gustavus's. What do you think happened to that deluded harpy? Is she dead?'

Rose had been respectfully staring at the carpet, but now she looked up at him sharply. 'That thing ate her! You said she'd gone. She must be dead. She has to be!' Rose exclaimed, staring at him, torn between hope and fear. 'But you don't think she is, do you?' she added quietly.

Mr Fountain stared up at the ceiling, at the pretty plaster mouldings. He twirled the ends of his moustache with a finger. 'I suspect not...' he said slowly. Then he glanced back at Rose and Freddie. 'I'm sorry. You were very clever – particularly using the elemental spirit, Frederick, that was positively inspired, as you had very little else to call on. Not many magicians have dealt with the things, either. Miss Sparrow might never have seen one before, although I had told her about my research.' He tugged his moustache angrily, and flinched. 'And about who knows what else. The woman's glamours were extraordinary. Let us hope she *is* dead, or at least somewhere beyond help. But we can't count on it, I'm afraid. She was so strong. I do wonder...' He sighed.

'What?' Rose, Freddie and Gustavus snapped

together, and Mr Fountain looked at them in surprise, as though he'd almost forgotten they were there.

'Ah. Well, I wonder if she might retain some of her own strength within the elemental force.'

Rose frowned. 'But…it ate her,' she pleaded.

'She was very strong,' Freddie agreed, sitting down rather heavily on an ottoman. 'She might have fought back.'

'You said all her power was in the glamours!' Rose rounded on Gus, who had leaped onto the ottoman too, and was now washing his ears in the way of a cat who wants to be busy.

'Mmmpf. So it was. But even an elemental spirit might be changed if it consumed all that magic,' he murmured in between swipes of his paw.

'So she's coming back.' Rose subsided onto the ottoman next to them. 'It was all for nothing.'

'Rose!' Mr Fountain sat up swiftly, and caught her chin, holding her face up to glare into her eyes. 'How can you say that? Look at them.' He turned her face to stare at the children soaking up the firelight. 'You, Freddie, my own daughter. All these other sons and daughters. People's children! You brought them back.'

'Actually, a lot of them are orphans,' Rose whispered.

'Sons and daughters once, and still precious,' Mr Fountain said sternly. 'All life is precious.' He turned her to face him once more, and gazed at them all with troubled eyes. 'Strange though it sounds, I'm almost relieved you didn't kill Alethea Sparrow. You think you'd be glad now, but killing people weighs on you. Even if there are reasons that seem too good to be denied. You're too young to have killed someone, both of you.'

Gus yawned, showing his very long teeth, and stood up, stepping delicately onto Rose's lap. 'Rose, dear,' he mewed plaintively. 'Interesting as this philosophical discussion is, I haven't eaten since those rather squashed fishpaste sandwiches.' He butted her chin affectionately, his face like bristly velvet. 'Don't worry, dear girl. Even if she does come back, it won't be for a while. You've got time to learn how to get her for good.'

Rose stared at him, and couldn't help smiling. For a moment she'd forgotten that she was going to be allowed to do more than clean the workroom. She was going to be Mr Fountain's apprentice. Even if Freddie was bound to make her do all the most boring bits of the spells for months and months. She hugged Gus gratefully, and stood up, dropping Mr Fountain a last awkward curtsey around Gus's solid furry body.

'Excuse me, Sir,' she murmured politely. 'I have to feed the cat.'

Don't miss the next
magical adventure with Rose...

ROSE

and the Lost Princess

Turn the page to read an extract!

Outside the palace, Mr Fountain's coachman let down the carriage steps, and Rose got down first to help Bella and Miss Anstruther out.

Bella looked over at the door as she jumped down, and frowned. 'Why's no one waiting for us? Usually there's a page on the steps, waiting to take me up to the Princesses' rooms.' Bella looked quite put out. She had been looking forward to showing off to Rose, for the page would have recognised her, and led her straight into the palace.

Instead of a page, two very large guardsmen with ceremonial pikes were standing one on either side of the door, their faces frozen.

'What do we do now?' Freddie hissed. The guardsmen looked almost twice as tall as he was.

'I don't know!' Bella muttered back. 'Usually they just stay there like that. I always want to pinch them to see if they'll do anything.'

'Don't!' Freddie yipped.

'Miss Anstruther!' Bella demanded.

Her governess was hunting through her bag distractedly, and didn't seem to have noticed that they hadn't been met. 'Yes, Isabella, dear?'

'What do we do? No one's here to meet us.'

Everyone stared at Miss Anstruther. Rose thought

that even one of the guards swivelled his eyes hopefully in her direction.

Miss Anstruther looked vague. 'Oh… Well, perhaps we should just go in – you know your way…'

Bella, Freddie and Rose formed a neat line behind the governess, and Bella pushed her gently up the steps. At the top, Miss Anstruther reached out for the door handle, and squeaked with dismay as the guardsmen's pikes slammed down in front of her. Clearly they were not so ceremonial after all.

'That's my governess! You can't spear my governess!' Bella squeaked indignantly. Only she was allowed to torture Miss Anstruther.

'No entry,' one of the guards intoned flatly, but he did look rather worried. Disembowelling governesses probably did not form part of his usual duties.

Miss Anstruther chose that moment to keel over backwards down the steps, most unfortunately flashing the guards with several lace-edged petticoats and her drawers. She also fell on Freddie and Rose.

'Oh, pick her up!' Bella snapped, stamping one little button-booted foot. Miss Anstruther had missed her, probably out of a well-developed sense of self-protection. 'Yes, you! How dare you assault my governess? My father is the Chief Magical Counsellor to the Treasury! He will turn you into coins!'

'Help!' Freddie moaned feebly. 'Can't breathe!'

Rose wriggled out from underneath Miss Anstruther's stiff bombazine skirts, and tried to tug the governess up again to rescue Freddie.

'Help us!' Bella smacked one of the guards in the leg, and went to haul Miss Anstruther's other hand.

The soldiers exchanged worried glances, and clearly decided that Bella was a more present danger than being court-martialled for abandoning their post. They stepped down to help pick up the dead weight of the collapsed governess.

'Better get her inside,' one of them muttered. 'Ask one of the stewards where to put her. Or get that idiot equerry that was hanging around.'

'Raph again. Bound to be,' Freddie wheezed, as Miss Anstruther was lifted off him.

'Yes, the equerry is his cousin, you'd better find him,' Bella directed firmly.

The guards looked even more worried as they found that this gaggle of squashed children had important connections. One of them opened the door with a flourish, and the other dumped Miss Anstruther on to a spindly gold chair in the hallway.

Rose looked around. She was not impressed so far – surely a palace ought to be rather more organised than this? And she could hear shouting. One did not shout in a palace. Everything was supposed to be hushed and serene and beautiful. She'd imagined it rather like a swan, perfect on the top, but kicking away like mad underneath.

A group of soldiers ran past, looking anxious, with their swords drawn, and Rose stared at Freddie and Bella.

'Is it usually like this?' she whispered worriedly.

'No,' Freddie muttered. 'I do hope we haven't chosen to visit in the middle of a revolution. This is all your fault, Bella!'

'No one came through this door?' A much more grandly dressed soldier strode up to the guards, who stopped fanning Miss Anstruther with their handkerchiefs and tried to look as though they hadn't just deserted their posts.

'No, sir!'

'Who are these?' The officer glared at the gaggle of children, finally allowing his gaze to linger distastefully on Miss Anstruther, who whimpered slightly.

Bella was made of much sterner stuff. 'I am Isabella Fountain, and my papa is going to be extremely annoyed when I tell him about this!' she retorted. 'We are supposed to be going to tea with Princess Jane.'

The officer stared blankly at her, then gave a short bark of laughter. 'You find her, my dear, and you can have as much tea as you want.' Wearily he rubbed a gloved hand, encrusted with gold braid, across his face.

Everyone stared at him.

'You've lost the princess?' Freddie whispered in horror.

The soldier went white as he realised what he'd done. 'Certainly not,' he snapped. 'And anyone spreading rumours to that effect will be guilty of incitement, and revolution, and other…very bad things.' He glared at Freddie. 'Her Royal Highness is indisposed, and won't be taking tea. A lady-in-waiting will write to you, I'm sure.'

There was a flurry of red and gold, and somehow they were all outside the door again, with William the coachman leaning against the carriage door and staring at them with his mouth open.

'They have!' Freddie murmured, staring at the firmly closed door. 'They've lost Princess Jane!'

Look out for
Rose and the Lost Princess
to find out what happens next!

Look out for the third magical
adventure with Rose...

ROSE
and the Magician's Mask

A precious mask of unimaginable power
has been stolen from the royal palace.
Rose suspects that dark magicians are at
work – and that danger looms...

The race to stop the evil thieves will take
Rose to the mysterious city of Venice, where
nothing is quite what it seems...
Can Rose use her magic to find the terrible
mask, before its true powers are revealed?